THE STONE BOOK QUARTET

ALAN · GARNER

THE STONE BOOK QUARTET

The Stone Book • *Granny Reardun*
The Aimer Gate • *Tom Fobble's Day*

HarperCollins
An Imprint of HarperCollins*Publishers*

First published in collected edition 1983
This edition 1992
Reprinted 1992

The Stone Book © Alan Garner 1976
Granny Reardun © Alan Garner 1977
The Aimer Gate © Alan Garner 1978
Tob Fobble's Day © Alan Garner 1977

The author asserts the moral right to be
identified as the author of this work

ISBN   0 00 184 289 7

CONTENTS

For Ralph Elliott

The Stone Book

THE
STONE BOOK

A bottle of cold tea; bread and a half onion. That was Father's baggin. Mary emptied her apron of stones from the field and wrapped the baggin in a cloth.

The hottest part of the day was on. Mother lay in bed under the rafters and the thatch, where the sun could send only blue light. She had picked stones in the field until she was too tired and had to rest.

Old William was weaving in the end room. He had to weave enough cuts of silk for two markets, and his shuttle and loom rattled all the time, in the day and the night. He wasn't old, but he was called Old William because he was deaf and hadn't married. He was Father's brother.

He carried the cuts to market on his back. Stockport was further, but the road was flatter. Macclesfield was nearer, but Old William had to climb Glaze Hill behind the cottage to get to the road. The markets were on Tuesday and Friday, and so he was weaving and walking always: weave and walk. "Then where's time for wedding?" he used to say.

Mary opened the door of Old William's room. "Do you want any baggin?" she said. She didn't speak, but moved her lips to shape the words.

"A wet of a bottle of tea," said Old William. He didn't speak, either. The loom was too loud. Mary and Old William could talk when everybody else was making a noise.

"Is it sweet?" he said.

"Yes. I made it for Father."

"Where's he working?"

"Saint Philip's," said Mary.

"Haven't they finished that steeple yet?" said Old William.

"He's staying to finish. They want it for Sunday."

"Tell him to be careful, and then. There's many another Sunday."

Old William was careful. Careful with weaving, careful carrying. He had to be. The weight could break his back if he fell on the hill.

"Mother!" Mary shouted up the bent stairs. "I'm taking Father his baggin!"

She walked under the trees of the Wood Hill along the edge of Lifeless Moss.

The new steeple on the new church glowed in the sun: but something glinted. The spire, stone like a needle, was cluttered with the masons' platforms that were left. All the way under the Wood Hill Mary watched the golden spark that had not been there before.

She reached the brick cottage on the brink of the Moss. Between there and the railway station were the houses that were being built. The railway had fetched a lot of people to Chorley. Before, Father said, there hadn't been enough work. But he had made gate posts, and the station walls, and the bridges and the Queen's Family Hotel; and he had even cut a road through rock with his chisel, and put his mark on it. Every mason had his mark, and Father put his at the back of a stone, or on its bed, where it wouldn't spoil the facing. But when he cut the road on the hill he put his mark on the face once, just once, to prove it.

Then Chorley must have a church next, and a school.

Father had picked the site for the quarry at the bottom of the Wood Hill. Close by the place, at the road, there was stone to be seen, but it was the soft red gangue that wouldn't last ten years of weather. Yet Father had looked at the way the trees grew, and had felt the earth and the leaf-mould between his fingers, and had said they must dig there. And there they had found the hard yellow-white dimension stone that was the best of all sands for building.

The beech trees had been cleared over a space, and two loads of the big branches had saved them coals at home for a year. It was one of the first memories of her life; the rock bared and cut by Father, and silver bark in the fire.

Now the quarry seemed so small, and the church so big. The quarry would fit inside a corner of the church; but the stone had come from it. People said it was because Father cut well, but Father said that a church was only a bit of stone round a lot of air.

Mary stood at the gate and looked up. High clouds moving made the steeple topple towards her.

"Father!"

She could hear his hammer, tac, tac, as he combed the stone.

The golden spark was a weathercock. It had been put up that week, and under its spike was the top platform. Father's head showed over the edge of the platform.

"Below!" His voice sounded nearer than he looked.

"I've brought your baggin!" Mary shouted.

"Fetch it, then!"

"All the way?"

"Must I come down when I'm working?"

"But what about the Governor?" said Mary.

"He's gone! I'm the Governor of this gang! There's only me stayed to finish! Have you the tea?"

"Yes!"

"Plenty of sugar?"

"Yes!"

"I can't spit for shouting! Come up!"

Mary hitched her frock and put the knot of the baggin cloth between her teeth and climbed the first ladder.

The ladders were spiked and roped, but the beginning of the steeple was square, a straight drop, and the ladders clattered on the side. She didn't like that.

"Keep fast hold of that tea!" she heard Father call, but she didn't lift her head, and she didn't look down.

Up she went. It felt worse than a rock because it was so straight and it had been made. Father had made parts of it. She knew the pattern of his combing hammer on the sandstone.

Up she went.

"Watch when you change to the spire!" Father's voice sounded no nearer.

At the spire, the pitch of the ladders was against the stone, and Mary had to step sideways to change. The ladders were firmer, but she began to feel a breeze. She heard an engine get up steam on the railway. The baggin cloth kept her mouth wet, but it felt dry.

The spire narrowed. There were sides to it. She saw the shallow corners begin. Up and up. Tac, tac, tac, tac, above her head. The spire narrowed. Now she couldn't stop the blue sky from showing at the sides. Then land. Far away.

Mary felt her hands close on the rungs, and her wrists go stiff.

Tac, tac, tac, tac. She climbed to the hammer. The spire was thin. Father was not working, but giving her a rhythm. The sky was now inside the ladder. The ladder was broader than the spire.

Father's hand took the baggin cloth out of Mary's mouth, and his other hand steadied her as she came up through the platform.

The platform was made of good planks, and Father had lashed them, but it moved. Mary didn't like the gaps between. She put her arms around the spire.

"That was a bonny climb," said Father.

"I do hope the next baby's a lad," said Mary.

"Have some tea," said Father.

She drank from the bottle. The cold sweet drink stopped her trembling.

"Don't look yet," said Father. "And when you do, look away first, not near. How's Mother?"

"Resting. She could only do five hours at the picking today, it got that hot."

"That's why I've stayed," said Father. "They want us to finish for Sunday, and there's one more dab of capping to do. There may be a sixpence for it."

"Doesn't it fear you up here?" said Mary.

"Now why should it?" said Father. "Glaze Hill's higher."

"But you can't fall off Glaze Hill," said Mary. "Not all at once."

"There's nothing here to hurt you," said Father. "There's stone, and wood and rope, and sky, same as at home. It's the same ground."

"It's further," said Mary.

"But it'll never hurt. And I'll go down

with you. Down's harder."

"I hope the next one's a lad," said Mary. "I'm fed up with being a lad – Father! See at the view! Isn't it!"

Mary stood and looked out from the spire. "And the church," she said. "It's so far away." She knelt and squinted between the planks. "The roof's as far as the ground. We're flying."

Father watched her; his combing hammer swung from his arm.

"There's not many who'll be able to say they've been to the top of Saint Philip's."

"But I'm not at the top," said Mary.

The steeple cap was a swelling to take the socket for the spike of the golden cockerel. Mary could touch the spike. Above her the smooth belly raced the clouds.

"You're not frit?"

"Not now," said Mary. "It's grand."

Father picked her up. "You're really not frit? Nobody's been that high. It was reared from the platform."

"Not if you help me," said Mary.

"Right," said Father. "He could do with a testing. Let's see if he runs true."

Father lifted Mary in his arms, thick with work from wrist to elbow. For a moment again the steeple wasn't safe on the earth when she felt the slippery gold of the weathercock bulging over her, but she kicked her leg across its back, and held the neck.

"Get your balance," said Father.

"I've got it," said Mary.

The swelling sides were like a donkey, and behind her the tail was stiff and high. Father's head was at her feet, and he could reach her.

"I'm set," she said.

Father's face was bright and his beard danced. He took off his cap and swept it in a circle and gave the cry of the summer fields.

"Who-whoop! Wo-whoop! Wo-o-o-o!"

Mary laughed. The wind blew on the spire and made the weathercock seem alive. The feathers of its tail were a marvel.

Father twisted the spike with his hands

against the wind, and the spike moved in its greased socket, shaking a bit, juddering, but firm. To Mary the weathercock was waking. The world turned. Her bonnet fell off and hung by its ribbon, and the wind filled her hair.

"Faster! Faster!" she shouted. "I'm not frit!" She banged her heels on the golden sides, and the weathercock boomed.

"Who-whoop! Wo-whoop! Wo-o-o-o!" cried Father. The high note of his voice crossed parishes and townships. Her hair and her bonnet flew, and she felt no spire, but only the brilliant gold of the bird spinning the air.

Father swung the tail as it passed him. "Who-whoop! Wo-whoop! Wo-o-o-o! There's me tip-top pickle of the corn!"

Mary could see all of Chorley, the railway and the new houses. She could have seen home but the Wood Hill swelled and folded into Glaze Hill between. She could see the cottage at the edge of Lifeless Moss, and the green of the Moss, and as she spun she could see Lord Stanley's, and Stockport and Wales, and Beeston and Delamere, and all to the hills and Manchester. The golden twisting spark with the girl on top, and everywhere across the plain were churches.

"Churches! I can see churches!"

And all the weathercocks turned in the wind.

Father let the spike stop, and lifted her down.

"There," he said. "You'll remember this day, my girl. For the rest of your life."

"I already have," said Mary.

Father ate his baggin. Mary walked round the platform. She looked at the new vicarage and the new school by the new church.

"Are you wishing?" said Father.

"A bit," said Mary. "I'm wishing I'd went.'

"It'd be fourpence a week, and all the time you'd have lost."

"I could have read," said Mary. "You can read."

She sat with her back against the steeple in its narrow shade. Glaze Hill was between her boots. "Have you asked if Lord Stanley'll set me on?"

"Lord Stanley doesn't like his maids to read," said Father.

"But have you?"

"Wait a year."

"I'm fretted with stone picking," said Mary. "I want to live in a grand house, and look after every kind of beautiful thing you can think of: old things: brass."

"By God, you'll find stone picking's easier!" The onion dropped off Father's knife and thumb and floated down to the lawns of the church. It had so far to fall that there was time for it to wander in the air.

"We'd best fetch that," said Father, "The vicar won't have us untidy."

He put Mary on the ladder and climbed outside her. Just as the sky and the steeple were inside the ladder, Mary was inside Father's long arms that pushed him out from the rungs. He didn't help her, but she felt free and safe and climbed as if there was no sky, no stone, no height.

She ran across the lawn and picked up the onion. Bits of it had smashed off and she nibbled them.

She stood with Father and looked up. The spire still toppled under the clouds.

"She'll do," said Father, and slapped the stone. "Yet she'll never do."

"Why?" said Mary.

"She's no church, and she'll not be. You want a few dead uns against the wall for it to be a church."

"They'll come."

"Not here," said Father. "There's to be no burial ground. Just grass. And without you've some dead uns, it's more like Chapel than Church. Empty."

He ate his onion.

Mary went back to work. She looked at Saint Philip's when she got to Lifeless Moss. Father was nearly at the top again. His arms were straight. He climbed balanced out from the stone.

She dipped a pansion of water in the spring and took some up to Mother. Mother was sleeping, but her hair was flat with sweat.

Old William was sweating at his loom. It was all clack. He had to watch the threads, and he couldn't look to talk.

Mary worked till the sun was cool, then she carried her stones home and made the tea. She washed little Esther and put her to bed, and gave Mother her tea. Father came home.

"That's finished," he said. He sat quietly in his chair. He was always quiet when the work was done, church or wall or garden.

After tea, Father went to see Mother. They talked, and he played his ophicleide to her. He played gentle tunes, not the ones for Sunday.

Mary cleared the table and washed the dishes. And when she'd finished she cleaned the stones from the field. Old William smoked

half a pipe of tobacco before going back to
the loom.

"Is he playing?" said Old William.

"Yes," said Mary. "But not Chapel. Why
are we Chapel?"

"You'd better ask him," said Old William.
"I'm Chapel because it's near. I do enough
walking, without Sunday."

Father came down from playing his music.
He sat at the table with Mary and sorted the
stones she had picked that day with little
Esther. Most pickers left their stones on the
dump at the field end, but Mary brought the
best of hers home and cleaned the dirt off,
and Father looked at them. In the field they
were dull and heavy, and could break a
scythe; but on the table each one was something different. They were different colours
and different shapes, different in size and
feel and weight. They were all smooth cobbles.

"Why are we Chapel?" said Mary.

"We're buried Church," said Father.

"But why?"

"There's more call on music in Chapel," said Father.

"Why?"

"Because people aren't content with raunging theirselves to death from Monday to Saturday, but they must go bawling and praying and fasting on Sundays too."

"What's the difference between Church and Chapel?" said Mary.

"Church is Lord Stanley."

"Is that all?"

"It's enough," said Father. "When you cut stone, you see more than the parson does, Church or Chapel."

"Same as what?"

"Same as this." Father took a stone and broke it. He broke it cleanly. The inside was green and grey. He took one half and turned so that Mary couldn't see how he rubbed it. Mary had tried to polish stone, but a whole day of rubbing did no good. It was a stone-cutter's secret, one of the last taught. Father held the pebble inside his waistcoat, and whatever it was that he did was simple; a way of holding, or twisting. And the pebble came out with its broken face green and white flakes, shining like wet.

He gave the pebble to Mary.

"Tell me how those flakes were put together and what they are," he said. "And who made them into pebbles on a hill, and where that was a rock and when." He rummaged in the pile on the table, found a round, grey stone, broke it, turned away, held, twisted, rubbed. "There."

Mary cried out. It was wonderful. Father had polished the stone. It was black and full of light, and its heart was a golden, bursting sun.

"What is it?" said Mary.

"Ask the parson," said Father.

"But what is it really?"

"I can't tell you," said Father. "Once, when I was prenticed, we had us a holiday, and I walked to the sea. I left home at two in the morning. I had nothing but half an hour there. And I stood and watched all that water, and all the weeds and shells and creatures; and then I walked back again. And I've seen the like of what's in that pebble only in the sea. They call them urchins. Now you tell me how that urchin got in that flint, and how that flint got on that hill."

"Was it Noah's flood?" said Mary.

"I'm not saying. But parsons will tell you, if you ask them, that Heaven and Earth, centre and circumference, were created all together in the same instant, four thousand and four years before Christ, on October the twenty-third, at nine o'clock in the morning. They've got it written. And I'm asking parsons, if it was Noah's flood, where was the urchin before? How long do stones take to grow? And how do urchins get in stones? It's time and arithmetic I want to know. Time and arithmetic and sense."

"That's what comes of reading," said Old William. "You're all povertiness and discontent, and you'll wake Mother."

"And what are you but a little master?" said Father. "Weaving till all hours and nothing to show for what you've spent."

"I'm still a man with a watch in his pocket," said Old William. "I don't keep my britches up with string."

Mary slid under the table and held on to the flint. There was going to be a row. Father thought shouting would make Old William hear, and Old William didn't have Father's words. Old William's clogs began to move as if he was working the loom, and Father's boots became still as if there was a great stone in his lap. Although he shouted, anger made him calm. When he was so still he frightened Mary. It was worse when the stillness came from himself and his thoughts, without a row. Sometimes it lasted for days. Then he would go out and play his ophicleide around the farms, and sing, and ring his handbells, and use all his music for beer, and only Mother could fetch him home. That was what Mary feared the most, because beer took

Father beyond himself and left someone looking through his eyes.

"And what about the cost of candles?" said Old William. "Books are dear reading when you've bought them."

Mary held the flint and tried to imagine such a golden apple that was once a star beneath the sea.

"Get weaving," said Father, "or it's you'll be the poverty-knocker."

Old William's clogs went out. Father sat at the table, not even moving the stones. Then he stood up and walked into the garden. Mary waited. She heard him rattling the hoe and rake, and Old William started up his loom, but she could tell he was upset, because of the slow beat, "Plenty-of-time, plenty-of-time". She crawled from under the table and went out to the garden. Father was hoeing next to the rhubarb.

"If I can't learn to read, will you give me something instead?" said Mary.

"If it's not too much," said Father. "The

trouble with him is," he said, and jutted his clay pipe at Old William's weaving room, "he's as good as me, but can't ever see the end of his work. And I make it worse by building houses for the big masters who've taken his living. That's what it is, but we never say."

"If I can't read, can I have a book?"

Father opened his mouth and the clay pipe fell to the ground and didn't break. He looked at the pipe. "I have not seen a Macclesfield dandy that has fallen to the ground and not broken," he said. "And they don't last more than a threeweek." He turned the soil gently with his hoe and buried the pipe.

"What've you done that for?" said Mary. "They cost a farthing!"

"Well," said Father, "I reckon, what with all the stone, if I can't give a bit back, it's a poor do. Why a book?"

"I want a prayer book to carry to Chapel," said Mary. "Lizzie Allman and Annie Leah have them."

"Can they read?"

"No. They use them to press flowers."

"Well, then," said Father.

"But they can laugh," said Mary.

"Ay," said Father. He leant on the hoe and looked at Glaze Hill. "Go fetch a bobbin of bad ends; two boxes of lucifer matches and a bundle of candles – a whole fresh bundle. We're going for a walk. And tell nobody."

Mary went into the house to Old William's room. In a corner by the door he kept the bad ends wound on bobbins. They were lengths of thread that came to him knotted or too thick or that broke on the loom. He tied them together and wove them for Mother to make clothes from. Mary lifted a bobbin and took it out. She found the candles and the lucifer matches.

Father had put his tools away.

They went up the field at the back of the house and onto Glaze Hill. When they reached the top the sun was ready for setting. The weathercock on Saint Philip's was losing light, and woods stretched out.

"I can't see the churches," said Mary. "When we were up there this afternoon I could."

"That's because they're all of a height," said Father. "I told you Glaze Hill was higher."

Glaze Hill was the middle of three spurs of land. The Wood Hill came in from the right, and Daniel Hill from the left, and they met at the Engine Vein. The Engine Vein was a deep crevice in the rocks, and along it went the tramroad for the miners who dug galena, cobalt and malachite. The thump of the engine that pumped water out of the Vein could often be heard through the ground on different parts of the hill, when the workings ran close to the surface.

Now it was dusk, and the engine quiet. The tramroad led down to the head of the first stope, and there was a ladder for men to climb into the cave.

Mary was not allowed at the Vein. It

killed at least once every year, and even to go close was dangerous, because the dead sand around the edge was hard and filled with little stones that slipped over the crag.

Father walked on the sleepers of the tram-road down into the Engine Vein.

"It's nearly night," said Mary. "It'll be dark."

"We've candles," said Father.

There was a cool smell, and draughts of sweet air. The roof of the Vein began, and they were under the ground. Water dripped from the roof onto the sandstone, splashing echoes. The drops fell into holes. They had fallen for so many years in the same place that they had worn the rock. Mary could get her fingers into some of the holes, but they were deeper than her hands.

Above and behind her, Mary saw the last of the day. In front and beneath was the stope, where it was always night.

Father took the whole bundle of candles and set them on the rocks and lit them. They showed how dark it was in the stope.

"Wait while you get used to it," said Father. "You soon see better. Now what about that roof?"

Mary looked up into the shadows. "It's not dimension stone," she said. "There's a grain to it, and it's all ridge and furrow."

"But if you'd been with me that day," said Father, "when I was prenticed and walked to the sea, you'd have stood on sand just the same as that. The waves do it, going back and to. And it makes the ridges proper hard, and if you left it I reckon it could set into stone. But the tide goes back and to, back and to, and wets it. And your boots sink in and leave a mark."

"If that's the sea, why's it under the ground?" said Mary.

"And whose are those boots?" said Father.

There were footprints in the roof, flattening the ripples, as though a big bird had walked there.

"Was that Noah's flood, too?" said Mary.

"I can't tell you," said Father. "If it was, that bantam never got into the ark."

"It must've been as big as Saint Philip's cockerel," said Mary.

"Bigger," said Father. "And upside down."

"It doesn't make sense," said Mary.

"It would if we could plunder it deep enough," said Father. "I reckon that if you're going to put the sea in a hill and turn the world over and let it dry, then you've got to be doing before nine o'clock in the morning. But preachers aren't partial to coming down here, so it doesn't matter. Does it?"

He blew out all the candles except two. He gave one to Mary and stepped onto the ladder. Mary went with him, and climbed between his arms down into the stope.

"It'd take some plucking," she said.

"If it had feathers."

The stope was the shape of a straw beehive and tunnels led everywhere. Mary couldn't see the top of the ladder.

"If you'd fallen, you'd have been killed

dead as at Saint Philip's," said Father.

"It's different," said Mary. "There's no height."

"There's depth, and that's no different than height," said Father.

"It doesn't call you," said Mary.

Father held Mary's hand sailor's grip and went into a tunnel under a ledge at the bottom of the stope. They didn't go far. There was a shaft in the rock, not a straight one, but when Father bridged it with his feet, the pebbles rattled down for a long time. It was easy climbing, even with a candle to be held, because the rock kept changing, and each change made a shelf. There was puddingstone, marl and foxbench, and only the marl was slippery.

"That's it," said Father. They were at a kink in the shaft.

"What about further down?" said Mary.

"It's only rubbish gangue from here to the bottom; neither use nor ornament. Although there was a man, him as sank this shaft, and he could read books and put a letter together. But he lost his money, for all his reading. Now if he'd read rocks instead of books, it might have been a different story, you see."

Father held his candle out to the side. There was a crack, not a tunnel. The rock itself had made it.

"Hold fast to your light," said Father. "And keep the matches out of the wet."

Father had to crawl. Mary could stand, but even she had to squeeze, because of the narrowness.

The crack went up and down, wavering through the hill. Then Father stopped. He couldn't turn his head to speak, but he could crouch on his heel. "Climb over," he said.

Mary pulled herself across his back. A side of wall had split off and jammed in the passage, almost closing it.

"Can you get through there?" said Father.

"Easy," said Mary.

"Get through and then listen," said Father.

Mary wriggled past the flake and stood up. The passage went on beyond her light. Father's candle made a dark hole of where she had come, and she could see his boots and one hand. He pushed the bobbin of bad ends through to her, and six candles. He kept hold of the loose end of silk.

"What's up?" said Mary. "What are we doing?"

"You still want a book for Sundays?" said Father. "Even if you can't read?"

"Yes," said Mary.

"Then this is what we're doing," said Father. "So you listen. You're to keep the lucifers dry, and use only one candle. It should be plenty. Let the silk out, but don't pull on it, else it'll snap. It's to fetch you back if you've no light, and that's all it's for. Now then. You'll find you go down a bit of steep, and then the rock divides. Follow the malachite. Always follow the malachite. Do you understand me?"

"Yes, Father."

"After the malachite there's some old fox-bench, then a band of white dimension, and a lot of wet when you come to the Tough Tom. Can you remember it all?"

"Malachite, foxbench, dimension, Tough Tom," said Mary.

"Always follow the malachite," said Father. "And if there's been another rockfall, don't trust loose stuff. And think on: there isn't anybody can reach you. You're alone."

"What must I do when I get to the Tough Tom?" said Mary.

"You come back and tell me if you want that book," said Father. "And if you do, you shall have it."

"Right," said Mary.

The crack in the hill ran straight for a while and was easier than the first part. She held her candle in one hand and the bobbin in the other. She had tucked the other candles and the lucifer matches into her petticoat. She went slowly down the rock, and the silk unwound behind her.

The steep was not enough to make her climb, and water trickled from above, over the rock, and left a green stain of malachite. She stopped when the passage divided, but there was nothing to worry her. She went to the left, with the malachite. The other passage had none.

She took the silk through the hill. The green malachite faded, and she passed by a thin level of foxbench sand, hard and speckled.

Then the walls were white. She was at the dimension. The crack sloped easily downward and was opening. She no longer had to move sideways. Her feet scuffed in the sand, but in front of her she could see brown water.

Mary held her candle low. At the bottom of the wall she saw the beginning of a band of clay, the Tough Tom red marl that never let water through. She went forward slowly into the wet. The floor was stiff and tacky under her boots, and behind her the silk floated in curves. But the crack went no deeper. The ground was level, and her light showed a hump of Tough Tom above the water, glistening.

Mary stopped again. There was nothing else, over, behind, below; only the Tough Tom humping out of the water, and the white dimension stone. And the crack finished at the end of her candlelight.

"Father!"

There was no reply. She hadn't counted how much silk had unwound.

"Father!"

There was plenty of candle left, but it showed her nothing to explain why she was there.

"Father!"

Not even an echo. There wasn't the room for one. But she turned. There hadn't been an echo, but her voice had sounded louder beyond the Tough Tom.

Mary scrambled up the hump, slithering in the wet. Then she looked around her, and saw.

The end of the crack was as broad as two stalls and as high as a barn. The red Tough Tom was a curved island above its own water. The walls were white and pale yellow. There was no sound. The water did not drip. It sank through the stone unheard, and seeped along the marl.

Mary saw Father's mason mark drawn on the wall. It was faint and black, as if drawn with soot. Next to it was an animal, falling. It had nearly worn itself away, but it looked like a bull, a great shaggy bull. It was bigger than it seemed at first, and Father's mark was on it, making the mark like a spear or an arrow.

The bull was all colours, but some of the stone had shed itself in the damp air. The more Mary looked, the bigger the bull grew. It had turned around every wall, as if it was moving and dying.

Mary had come through the hill to see Father's mark on a daubed bull. And near the bull and the mark there was a hand, the outline of a hand. Someone had splayed a hand on the wall and painted round it with the Tough Tom. Fingers and thumb.

Mary put the candle close. A white dimension hand. She lifted her own and laid it over the hand on the wall, not touching. Both hands were the same size. She reached nearer. They were the same size. She touched. The rock was cold, but for a moment it had almost felt warm. The hands fitted. Fingers and thumb and palm and a bull and Father's mark in the darkness under the ground.

Mary stood back, in the middle of the Tough Tom, and listened to the silence. It was the most secret place she had ever seen. A bull drawn for secrets. A mark and a hand alone with the bull in the dark that nobody knew.

She looked down. And when she looked down she shouted. She wasn't alone. The Tough Tom was crowded. All about her in that small place under the hill that led nowhere were footprints.

They were the footprints of people, bare and shod. There were boots and shoes and clogs, heels, toes, shallow ones and deep ones, clear and sharp as if made altogether, trampling each other, hundreds pressed in the clay where only a dozen could stand. Mary was in a crowd that could never have been, thronging, as real as she was. Her feet made prints no fresher than theirs.

And the bull was still dying under the mark, and the one hand still held.

There was nowhere to run, no one to hear. Mary stood on the Tough Tom and waited. She daren't jerk the thread to feel Father's presence; he was so far away that the thread would have broken.

Then it was over. She knew the great bull on the rock enclosing her, and she knew the mark and the hand. The invisible crowd was not there, and the footprints in the Tough Tom churned motionless.

She had seen. Now there was the time to go. Mary lifted the thread and made skeins of it as she went past the white dimension, foxbench and malachite to the candle under the fall.

Father had moved to make room for her.

"Well?"

"I've seen," said Mary. "All of it."

"You've touched the hand?"

"Yes."

"I thought you would."

They went back to the shaft, and up, and out. The sky seemed a different place. All things led to the bull and the mark and the hand in the cave. Trees were trying to find it with their roots. The rain in the clouds must fall to the ground and into the rock to the Tough Tom.

"That's put a quietness on you," said Father.

"Ay."

They came over Glaze Hill.

"Why did you set your mark on?" said Mary.

"I didn't. It was there when I went."

"When did you go?"

"When I was about your size. My father took me same as today. We have to go before we're too big to get past the fall, though I reckon, years back, the road was open; if you knew it was there."

"When did you go last?" said Mary.

"We go just once," said Father. "So that we'll know."

"Who else?"

"Only us. Neither Leahs nor Allmans. Us."

"But there were ever so many feet," said Mary. "The place was teeming."

"We've been going a while," said Father.

"And that bull," said Mary.

"That's a poser. There's been none like it in my time; and my father, he hadn't seen any."

"What is it all?" said Mary.

"The hill. We pass it on: and once you've seen it, you're changed for the rest of your days."

"Who else of us?" said Mary.

"Nobody," said Father, "except me: and

now you: it's always been for the eldest: and from what I heard my father say, it was only ever for lads. But if they keep on stoping after that malachite the way they're going at the Engine Vein, it'll be shovelled up in a year or two without anybody noticing even. At one time of day, before the Engine Vein and that chap who could read books, we must have been able to come at it from the top. But that's all gone. And if the old bull goes, you'll have to tell your lad, even if you can't show him."

"I shall," said Mary.

"I recollect it puts a quietness on you, does that bull. And the hand. And the mark."

Mary went to wash the Tough Tom from her boots in the spring when they reached home. The spring came out of the hill and soaked into Lifeless Moss, and Lifeless Moss spilled by brooks to the sea.

Father sat with Mother for a while. Old William had picked up his usual rhythm, and the loom rattled, "Nickety-nackety, Monday-come-Saturday". Then Father collected his work tools and sat down at the table and sorted through the pebbles.

He weighed them in his hand, tested them on his thumbnail, until he found the one he wanted. He pushed the others aside, and he took the one pebble and worked quickly with candle and firelight, turning, tapping, knapping, shaping, twisting, rubbing and making, quickly, as though the stone would set hard if he stopped. He had to take the picture from his eye to his hand before it left him.

"There," said Father. "That'll do."

He gave Mary a prayer book bound in blue-black calf skin, tooled, stitched and decorated. It was only by the weight that she could tell it was stone and not leather.

"It's better than a book you can open," said Father. "A book has only one story. And tomorrow I'll cut you a brass cross and let it in the front with some dabs of lead, and then I'll guarantee you'd think it was Lord Stanley's, if it's held right."

"It's grand," said Mary.

"And I'll guarantee Lizzie Allman and Annie Leah haven't got them flowers pressed in their books."

Mary turned the stone over. Father had split it so that the back showed two fronds of a plant, like the silk in skeins, like the silk on the water under the hill.

And Father went out of the room and left Mary by the fire. He went to Old William and took his ophicleide, as he always did after shouting, and he played the hymn that Old William liked best because it was close to the beat of his loom. William sang for the rhythm, "Nickety-nackety, Monday-come-Saturday", and Father tried to match him on the ophicleide.

William bawled:

 " 'Oh, the years of Man are the looms
   of God
 'Let down from the place of the sun;
 'Wherein we are weaving always,
 'Till the mystic work is done!' "

And so they ended until the next time. The last cry went up from the summer fields, "Who-whoop! Wo-whoop! Wo-o-o-o!"

And Mary sat by the fire and read the stone book that had in it all the stories of the world and the flowers of the flood.

GRANNY REARDUN

GRANNY REARDUN

They were flitting the Allmans. Joseph sat at the top of Leah's Bank and watched.

The horse and cart stood outside the house, by the field gate. Elijah Allman lifted the dollytub onto the cart first and set it in the middle. Then Alice and Amelia climbed into the dollytub, and Elijah packed them round with bedding. Young Herbert was carrying chairs.

The Allmans loaded the cart with furniture, stacking from the girls in the dollytub, so that the load was firm. Mrs Allman
came out of the house backwards on her
knees. She was donkey-stoning the doorstep
white, and when she had done she stood up,
and reached over the step and pulled the
door to.

Elijah helped her up onto the carter's
seat. Young Herbert sat next to her, holding
the reins. Elijah took the bridle and walked
the horse through the field gateway, down
the Hough and onto the Moss.

Joseph listened to them go. He went to
the top corner post of the field, ran three
strides and slid down Leah's Bank. It was
such a steep hill, and the grass so hard and
slippery, that he could slide for yards at a
time, standing. And when the grass was
brogged by old cow muck, he had only to
keep his balance, skip, and be away again.

He pushed the door open.

The house smelt wet with donkey-stone
and limewash. The rooms were enormous

empty. All the floors were white, all the walls and beams and the ceilings white. The stairs were sand-scoured, and the boards too. There was no dirt anywhere.

Joseph looked out of the bedroom window. The Allmans were away across the Moss. He left the house and went home for breakfast. He lived at the bottom of the hill.

Grandfather had finished his breakfast and was smoking a pipe of tobacco in his chair by the fire. His hard fingers could press the tobacco down hot in the bowl, without burning himself.

"They've flitted Allmans," said Joseph.

"Ay," said Grandfather.

"What for?" said Joseph.

"The years they've been there," said Grandfather. "It's a wonderful thing, them in their grandeur, and us in raddle and daub."

"Why?" said Joseph.

"Eat your pobs," said Grandmother.

Grandfather knocked the ashes of his pipe

out onto his hand and pitched them in the fire. He raised himself. "Best be doing," he said. "Damper Latham's getting for me. And think on," he said to Joseph, "I'll have half an hour from you before school. Is your mother coming up for her dinner today?"

"And fetching Charlie," said Joseph. "She promised."

Grandfather picked up his canvas bass and took his cap off the doornail. The chisels and hammers clinked together in the bass. "Be sharp," he said to Joseph.

Grandfather was old. But he still turned out. He was building a wall into the hedge bank of Long Croft field, down the road from the house, under the wood.

Joseph washed his basin and spoon at the spring in the garden, and ran down the road to Long Croft.

Grandfather was rough-dressing the stone for the wall, and laying it out along the hedge. Joseph unwound the line and pegged one end in the joints where Grandfather had finished the day before, and pulled the line tight against the bank. His job was to cut the bank back to receive the stone and to run a straight bed for the bottom course.

He chopped at the bank.

"Sweep up behind you," said Grandfather. "Muck's no use on the road. It wants to be on the field."

Joseph had to throw the clods high over his head to clear the quickthorn hedge.

"Get your knee aback of your shovel," said Grandfather. "There's no sense in mauling yourself half to death. Come on, youth. Shape!"

Joseph chopped, shovelled and threw. Grandfather worked the stone.

"I don't know why I bother," he said. "I'd as lief let it lie. The rubbish they send! I doubt there's not above a hundred years in it. Watch your line!"

Joseph was sweating. Grandfather took the spade from him and looked along the bank. He walked down the raw cut edge and shaved the earth with light swings of the blade. "You've got it like a fiddler's elbow," he said.

Damper Latham came with his cart up the road under the wood from Chorley. The cart was heavy and pulled by two Shires. Their brasses glinted. Suns, moons and clovers chimed on their leathers. Damper Latham kept his horses smart as a show.

"Now then, Robert," he said.

Grandfather looked over the side of the cart. "What's all this?" he said. "It's never stone."

Damper Latham winked at Joseph. "Eh, dear, dear! Robert?" he said. "Has the Missis been sitting on your shirt tail?"

"Take it away," said Grandfather. "I'll not put me name to it."

Damper Latham let down the boards and the sides of the cart and climbed onto the load. He began to walk the stones to the edge and slide them down two planks to Grandfather.

"You'll take what you're given, Robert," he said. "Else go without. I've had a job for to get these."

Grandfather grunted, and swung the blocks to lie as he wanted. They seemed to move without more than his hand on them.

Joseph tried to help, but he couldn't even pull the weight from the slope of the plank. He pulled and shoved, and the block shifted its balance and came at him. He couldn't stop it and he couldn't put it down and it was fighting him. He twisted away, but he still couldn't let go. The living dead weight of it all gripped his hands and wrenched his shoulders. Then it fell clear and smashed on the road.

"You great nowt!" shouted Grandfather. "See at what you've done!"

Joseph ran up the plank to the cart.

"See at it!" shouted Grandfather. "I can't use that! I'm not a man with string round his britches!"

The chapel clock struck eight.

"There's not better to be got, Robert," said Damper Latham.

"Well, I'll not abide it," said Grandfather.

"Must I go fetch you a load from Leah's

Bank?" said Damper Latham.

"No!"

"Where's stone on Leah's Bank?" said Joseph.

"It's eight o'clock," said Grandfather. "Time you were off."

"Stay and give us a tune," said Damper Latham. "I'm going down the village. You can have a ride."

"He'll be late," said Grandfather.

"He'll not," said Damper Latham. "The E-Flat's under me coat there."

Joseph picked up the bright cornet from beneath the seat and set his tongue to the mouthpiece and loosened the valves with his fingers.

"What must I play?" he said.

"Give us a Methody hymn for to fetch this load off," said Damper Latham. "One with a swing."

Joseph played "Man Frail and God Eternal" twice. Grandfather and Damper Latham worked together, as they had always done. The stone moved lightly for them.

"*The busy tribes of flesh and blood, with all their lives and cares,*" sang Damper Latham, "*are carried downwards by the flood, and lost in following years.*"

"Couldn't wait," said Grandfather. "One week to flit. Out."

"Where've they gone?" said Damper Latham.

"The Moss," said Grandfather.

"Give us a swing, youth!" Damper Latham nudged Joseph. Joseph had stopped playing.

"Let's have some Temperance," said Grandfather.

So Joseph played "Dip your Roll in your own Pot at Home".

"How's Elijah?" said Damper Latham.

"Badly," said Grandfather. "Them as can't bend, like as not they break."

"Eh," said Damper Latham, and he looked both ways on the road before he spoke. "Is it true what it's for? A kitchen garden?"

"True? It's true!" said Grandfather. "Kitchen garden! Rector's wife must grow herself a vine and a twothree figs, seemingly. She caught a dose of religion, that one; and there's Allmans out. Hey!"

Joseph was looking at his own stretched face in the swell of the cornet. Someone must have taken the brass and shaped it and turned it, with valves for every note, tapping, drawing it to soprano E-Flat.

"Hey! Let's hear 'Ode to Drink'. This lot wants some raunging." The cart shook as Grandfather pulled at the base of the stack.

Joseph sucked for spit, but his mouth had dried.

Grandfather and Damper Latham began without him, and he had to catch up when his lips were wet.

"Let thy devotee extol thee,
   And thy wondrous virtues sum;
But the worst of names I'll call thee,
   O thou hydra monster Rum!"

The stones thumped off.

"Pimple-maker, visage-bloater,
  Health-corrupter, idler's mate;
Mischief-breeder, vice-promoter,
  Credit-spoiler, devil's bait!"

Damper Latham swept the cart with his broom, and danced and marched to Joseph's music. Grandfather had his chisels out and was hitting the notes on them with his hammer, like a xylophone.

"Utterance-boggler, stench-emitter,
  Strong-man sprawler, fatal drop;
Tumult-raiser, venom-spitter,
  Wrap-inspirer, coward's prop!"

Joseph had stopped playing. His neck hurt for thought of the Allmans. He couldn't swallow. But Grandfather and Damper Latham went on, singing louder and louder, tenor and bass, by turns.

Joseph shut his eyes.

"Virtue-blaster, base deceiver!
  Spite-displayer, sot's delight!
Noise-exciter, stomach-heaver!
  Falsehood-spreader! Scorpion's bite!"

Grandfather and Damper Latham were laughing too much to work.

Joseph opened his eyes. He was looking straight into Grandfather's, and they were hard, fierce, kind and blue.

"That's it, youth," said Grandfather. "Skrike or laugh. You'll learn."

Damper Latham backed the cart round for the village. "Shall you be wanting anything, Robert?" he said.

"If you're going by the smithy, tell Jump I need a four-pounder. And tell him I'll see him."

"Right you are, Robert," said Damper Latham. "Coom-agen, coom-agen," he called to the horses, and the two Shires scraped sparks with their shoes, and pulled. Damper Latham nodded towards the brass cornet in Joseph's hands and went on singing, his head and shoulders going back and to like a big clock.

"Quarrel-plotter, rage-discharger,
Giant-conqueror, wasteful sway . . ."

Joseph picked up the tune again.

"Chin-carbuncler, tongue-enlarger!
Malice-venter, Death's broad way!"

Grandfather was singing, too, and striking the chisels. His voice and their ringing faded. Joseph played and played.

"Tempest-scatterer, window-smasher,
    Death-forerunner, hell's dire brink!
Ravenous murderer, windpipe-slasher,
    Drunkard's lodging, meat and drink!"

Damper Latham and Joseph rode in silence. After the music, the horses and the cart were a quietness.

"Your Grandfather: he was a bit upset, that's all," said Damper Latham. "It's hard, at his time of day."

"I know," said Joseph.

"After all the tremendous work he's done. And now I can't hardly get him enough red rubbish for a length of wall – him as has cut only the best dimension stone all these years. It comes very hard."

"He wants me to follow him," said

Joseph.

Damper Latham looked sideways quickly.

"And shall you?"

"No."

"What shall you do, then? Go for a brick-setter?"

"No. I don't know."

"When do you finish your schooling?"

"Today," said Joseph.

"And you're not prenticed?"

"Me Grandfather thinks I'll be with him. But I'll never," said Joseph.

"I've been getting for Robert thirty years," said Damper Latham. "And there isn't the call on it now. Everywhere's brick. They want setters, not getters."

Joseph looked at the brass cornet. "Is it correct about Allmans?"

"Ay."

"They've been put out?"

"Ay."

"For a garden wall?"

"Ay."

"What's wrong with bricks for a garden?" said Joseph.

"Wouldn't suit," said Damper Latham. "And that house is the last dimension in the Hough. They had to flit."

The Shires stopped without telling when they came to the smithy. Damper Latham hitched their reins and went into the farrier's yard and down the wide steps to the cellar where the forge stood. Joseph put the cornet back under the seat and followed, quietly.

The smith and all his gang were working in a red and black light, hammermen every one of them, and making things. The noise was tremendous.

"Now then, Jump!" shouted Damper Latham.

"Now then, Damper!" shouted the smith, and all the hammering and the noise stopped. Horseshoes quenched in the trough.

Joseph stayed back from the men, watching, near the bellows of the forge. The long handle of the bellows was above him in the shadow.

The gang sat down and drew their beer from a keg under the bench and gave Damper Latham his mug.

Joseph reached up and put his fingers round the bellows handle. The ashwood was like silk to touch. He gripped hold to feel, and the handle moved before he could stop it. It moved just once, down and up, and the bellows breathed, and the coals glowed.

The smith looked, and saw Joseph. Joseph kept hold of the handle.

"That'll do, youth," said the smith gently, but he meant it.

Joseph let go.

"Best be off," said Damper Latham.

Joseph turned away from the warmth and the busy men together, up the steps into the farrier's yard and daylight, and he went excited.

The chapel clock struck nine.

Joseph was late for school. He could hear

its bell ringing the scholars in. He looked up at the chapel spire. At opposite ends of the village stood the two great pieces of Grandfather's life: church and chapel. They marked the village for him. Saint Philip's had a bigger steeple, and the chapel had the clock.

Joseph walked down the village towards the school and Saint Philip's, over the station bridge. Everything he saw was clear. He knew something he didn't know. It was the bell. It was the clock. It was the spires!

Grandfather had worked the chapel, but he had not given it the time. He had helped on the school, but he couldn't ring them in. He had topped Saint Philip's steeple, but it wasn't the top. The top was a golden vane, a weather cock. Cock, clock, bell and at the chapel a spike to draw lightning. Wind, time, voice and fire – they were all the smith!

Joseph's palm sweated on the cold iron latch of the big school door. Inside the hall he heard the end of prayers.

The carpenter couldn't lock the door. The carpenter could never open it or close. Latch, lock, hinges were the smith.

Joseph looked down. The step was stone, and he would not cross it for his last day. Still holding, he faced about.

The school porch showed the view, a stone arch around the world, and Grand-father had made that. It framed Saint Philip's steeple and the weathercock.

And then Joseph knew.

That great steeple, that great work. It was a pattern left on sand and air. The glint of the sun from the weathercock shimmered his gaze, and the gleam was about the stone right to the earth. He saw golden brushes, the track of combing chisels, every mark. The stone was only the finish of the blow. The church was the print of chisels in the sky.

Joseph let go of the latch handle. Behind him was the step into the hall. In front of him was the step through the arch. Not even for his last day could he go to school. There was no time. He stood between stone and stone.

"No back bargains!" shouted Joseph, and did a standing leap through the arch. He fell over and rolled on the ground.

Joseph breathed in. The weathercock raced the clouds.

He walked away from the school, past the church, over the station bridge, towards the chapel clock. Nothing he saw or could think of went beyond the smith. Shoes on the horses, their bridles and brasses, the iron of the coach wheels, the planes, blades, adzes, axes, bradawls and bits led to the forge. Even the hands on the clock. Without that fire there was no time.

Joseph went into the farrier's yard and down to the cellar. The apprentice was working the bellows handle: up and down, and up and down. The cellar breathed.

Joseph stood quietly, just looking.

"What are you after, youth?"

The smith was behind him, at the top of the steps in the yard.

"Will you set me on?" said Joseph. "I'll be prenticed to you."

"Shall you?" said the smith. "Come up, then."

He was a big man, in his shirt sleeves; a leather brat, tied round his waist, reached below his knees. He bent and put his arms under the farrier's anvil, lifted it from its bed, carried it across the yard and set it down.

"Now take it back," he said to Joseph.

Joseph put his arms around the anvil and lifted. His chin jarred on the top. He tried again, firming his chin against the steel. Nothing moved. But it was not like stone; not like the rough dead weight that tore on Damper Latham's planks.

"I can't shift it," said Joseph.

"A smith carries his anvil."

"Well I can't yet."

"You can't shift an anvil," said the smith, "yet you want to join the generous, ingenious hammermen? You can't shift an anvil, but you want your own sledge?"

"I do," said Joseph.

"Then give me one reason why I should set you on," said the smith. "Why should I take me another prentice for six years of no gain? You're old Robert's lad, aren't you?"

"Ay."

"The granny reardun?"

"But me mother's coming up our house for her dinner."

"You're still a granny reardun."

Joseph said nothing.

"And what does Robert think?"

"I've not told him," said Joseph.

"Not told him? You're a previous sort of a youth, aren't you?"

"I've not had chance," said Joseph.

"Then you'd best make chance," said the smith. "And I'm still waiting to hear why I should put meself out to find sufficient meat, drink, apparel, washing and lodging for a prentice as can't shift his anvil."

"Because a smith's aback of everything," said Joseph.

"He's what did you say?"

"Aback of everything. He's master."

The smith went to a chest of drawers in the yard, opened the top drawer and took out a roll of parchment paper.

"Can you tell me what this is?" he said.

"It's called an Indenture," said Joseph.

"And an Indenture is a legal document," said the smith.

"I know," said Joseph.

"Binding you and me."

Joseph nodded.

"Can you read?" said the smith.

"Ay," said Joseph.

"Write?"

"Ay."

"Well, I'm beggared if I can," said the smith. "Anyroad: a prentice, it says here, is to be learned the art, craft and mystery of the forge."

Joseph felt as if everything around him had stopped but those words.

"And he shall faithfully serve the hammerman, his secrets keep, his lawful commands everywhere gladly obey."

Joseph put his hands between his knees, and listened.

"At cards, dice or any unlawful game he shall not play. He shall not absent himself, day or night, nor haunt ale houses, taverns or playhouses, commit fornication nor contract for matrimony."

"I'll not," said Joseph.

"You'll be a rum un if you don't," said the smith. "But that's it. That's what it says."

"I'll go tell me Grandfather now," said Joseph.

"When can you start?" said the smith.

"As soon as I've shifted this anvil," said Joseph.

"Wait on, now!" The smith laughed. "Robert and me must have us a proper weisening about you first." He picked up the anvil and firmed it back on its bed. "And that," he said, "you'll lift just before you're out of your time, because by then, youth, we'll have put some muscle on you. Now get off up home and tell your Grandfather. And take this four-pounder Damper Latham asked for."

He gave Joseph a steel hammer-head, blunt at one end, and sharp for splitting at the other, with a hole through it for its haft.

Joseph held it up. "See," he said. "It is aback of everything."

"Tell that to Robert!" said the smith. "And think on: you can play wag from school, but you'll not play wag from me."

Joseph walked below the chapel clock. He could hear its tick.

When he reached the wood he climbed up the slope among the beech trees, so that Grandfather wouldn't see him. He wanted to choose his moment. There was a lot of distant noise coming off Leah's Bank.

The road was empty. Grandfather was not at the wall, nor was he anywhere that Joseph could tell from the wood.

Joseph strode, slack-kneed, down through the leaf-mould of the hill. It was the way to move, even at night, so that roots and rocks wouldn't catch the feet and he kept the rhythm of the ground.

Grandfather's bass was tucked behind the field hedge. All his tools were there. Joseph put the new hammer-head with them.

"Where is he?" he said.

There was another load of stone dumped at the end of the run of wall, but it wasn't rubbish: it was square-cut white dimension, weathered, good. A barrow-load only.

"Grandfather!"

Some of the stone was white with lime-wash on one side. Joseph touched it. The lime was still wet.

"Grandfather!"

"Who-whoop!"

It was Grandfather's shout. It carried a mile on the hill, and Grandmother always used it to call him home.

"Wo-whoop! Wo-o-o-o!" answered Joseph.

"Who-whoop!" cried Grandfather some-where.

"Wo-whoop! Wo-o-o-o!"

"Who-whoop!"

Grandfather was coming from the house. He appeared over the road crest a hundred yards away. He walked strongly.

" 'Therefore, behold, I will hedge up thy way with thorns, and make a wall!' "

Grandfather knew the Bible whenever he was drunk.

" 'And I will destroy her vines and her fig trees! And I will make them a forest! And the beasts of the field shall eat them!' "

His eyes were bright and his face was a good colour. That was all. He stood and inspected the work he had done, and he lifted his cap and rubbed his forehead with the knuckle of his thumb.

"What a wall," said Grandfather. "Looks like it died in a fog."

Then he was splendid.

He took the new stone, the square dimension, and he built. He smoothed and combed the blocks, and they fitted together with hardly a knife-space between them. Their weight was nothing for him, and Joseph watched the old man happy.

The wall was being built. No limewash showed, no donkey-stoning. "There," said Grandfather.

"Why?" shouted Joseph. "Why've you taken it? Why you?"

"That's a poser," said Grandfather. "Eh up. Here's a new four-pounder in me little bass."

"Why?"

"You fetched it, I reckon. Or Damper Latham."

"The stone! Allmans' stone!"

"So it is," said Grandfather. "Ay. Young Herbert wheeled me a barrow-load. I could do with another."

"I'll not!" shouted Joseph, and ran.

He ran all the way home, up the garden path, through the doorway, up the bent stairs and fell on his bed under the limewash and the sloping thatch. He lay there, grasping the corner post of the house to hold the world. The lime flaked off the oak. It needed a new coat. And all the time there was the noise on Leah's Bank, a swearing, tearing noise, and dust from it finely settled his tears.

Joseph heard Mother come, and Charlie. The bassinet grated on the path. Charlie wanted his dinner, but Joseph couldn't go down to see him. There was that noise.

Grandmother and Mother went into the back garden to pick peas. Joseph waited until the inside of the downstairs was quiet, then he crept out.

Charlie was parked under the thatch away from the sun. He laughed at Joseph, and Joseph played with him. The bassinet was lop-sided because a spring had broken. Mother had brought it for Grandfather to mend.

Joseph helped shell the peas, and he gave the little ones to Charlie. Mother peeled the potatoes. It was going to be a big dinner.

"Have you played wag?" said Grandfather.

Joseph didn't answer.

"Well, you can go help Damper Latham this after," said Grandfather. "I've a flavour for to finish that wall."

"Where?" said Joseph.

"Long Croft, you pan-head."

"Where with Damper Latham?"

"Leah's Bank. Where else?"

"I'll not."

"And I'll catch you a clinker if I hear any more of that," said Grandfather. "Where's me dinner?" he shouted, and poured himself more beer.

Joseph fed Charlie, and played with him again. Grandfather fitted the haft to the new hammer-head and dropped it in the rain-butt to swell. Then he tied the bassinet together with rope.

"Put that Charlie of yours down," Grandfather said to Joseph. "Play wag at end of schooling, and you're half a day a man's lad. Let's be having you."

They went down the path together. The noise on the hill was no better.

"You get yourself up them fields and tell Damper Latham I've sent you. I'll ready the bank."

"Just why?" said Joseph.

Grandfather looked at him before he spoke. And when he did speak he was not drunk. There was no beer in him talking.

"Why," he said. "Why. Must I cut me nose off to spite me face?"

"But Allmans," said Joseph.

"Is it me making that racket yonder?" said Grandfather. "It is not. They've got allsorts there – men as couldn't tell foxbench from malachite. So what must I do? Let it go? Let it all go? For a garden? Or shall I have a word with the Governor, and slip him a sixpence? Eh? That garden wall will never be nothing. But all your days you'll pass the dimension by Long Croft, and you'll say, 'Ay, he was a bazzil-arsed old devil, but him and me, we built that!'"

And Joseph couldn't tell him.

They went to their work.

The house was terrible on Leah's Bank. Its roof and the gable ends were off. The stone slates had been sent down and stacked by size, Princesses, Duchesses, Small Countesses, Ladies, Wide Doubles and the neat Jenny-go-lightlies from under the ridge. The sheepbone pegs that had held them to the roof were scattered on the ground, as if the house was eaten.

Timbers had been sorted; common rafters, purlins, joists, trusses, wind-braces and bearers.

And Young Herbert Allman was day-labouring for the men.

The house was down to its eaves. Only the bedroom window stood higher, showing sky from both sides through its glass.

Young Herbert stopped his barrowing. He said nothing. He picked up Mrs Allman's donkey-stone from beside the dirtied step, lifted his arm and winged the donkey-stone straight to the pane. Then he still said nothing, and got on with his load.

Joseph took a lump of rubble from the wall-packing and watched the window. The broken pane was clean now.

He let go. The rock lobbed over and over and hit. The window burst with a sound that Joseph felt in his stomach. It was so good he did it again.

"And is that what a man's lad thinks of his first half-day?" said Damper Latham.

He was walking round the building to put his chalk mark on likely stone.

"Has Robert sent you?"

"He has," said Joseph.

"To chuck cob-ends at windows? You're a constructive sort of a youth, aren't you?"

"It's . . . them!" said Joseph.

"It's not," said Damper Latham. "It's you."

"I've not ridded Allmans! I've not wrecked this!"

"Give over gondering at what can't be helped," said Damper Latham.

Joseph pulled aside the stones that Damper Latham had marked. The noise around him was no less, and through it Young Herbert barrowed.

The stone was as heavy as before. Joseph's hands blistered.

Yet the anvil was heavier than stone, and the forge louder than the hill. But he wanted them. He wanted metals that could be made and the sounds of making. He could not forget the limewashed walls of the morning. For this.

"Tea up!" shouted the Governor. The men stopped, and squatted on the grass. Damper Latham gave Joseph a drink from his bottle. The sweetness calmed him. The hill was quiet. He knew where he was once more on Leah's Bank above his own house.

The sun caught movement at Long Croft field, reflection on a chisel, and the sound of Grandfather's hammer could just be heard, like a small bell.

Even the ruin was gentle now. It had its place.

"It was me," Joseph said to Damper Latham. "I was that upset."

"Ay."

"What's to become of it all?" said Joseph.

"Oh, not much," said Damper Latham. "They'll have the house down in the day. Then it'll go to nettles, a ruck of stones, and cussing every time Jesse Leah catches his scythe on a bit of a doorstep. But at after, and before you know, there'll be only meadow and a hump to it by a gate, and some damson tresses in a hedge without sense nor reason. And that's all. Now hadn't you ought go and tell him?"

"Who?"

"Your Grandfather."

"Tell him what?"

"About old Jump setting you on."

Joseph startled, and couldn't speak.

"You're gondering again, youth," said Damper Latham. "Well, is he or isn't he?"

"How did you hear?" said Joseph.

"Hear? Jump and me's had us eye on you this twelvemonth and more. It's in you."

"What is?"

"Smithing, of course!"

"In me," said Joseph.

"And it'll out, one road or the other," said Damper Latham. "Hinder, and you'll turn sour as verjuice."

"Does me Grandfather know?" said Joseph.

"There's not but one can face Robert with that news," said Damper Latham.

"Me?" said Joseph. Leah's Bank was hushed. Men went back to work, but the noise no longer hurt. Pick-axes, pinch-bars, crows, wedges, sledges battered and prized the house. Dust shimmered Joseph's gaze in the sun, and out of it he could remember before breakfast, and now see the track of picks, with stone the finish of the blow, and not all smithing was making.

"Me," said Joseph. "Me."

"I'll be along with the dimension in half an hour," said Damper Latham.

"I'll tell him I'll tell him I'll tell him!" shouted Joseph, and ran down Leah's Bank.

"I'll tell him I'll tell him I'll tell him. I'll tell him I'll tell him I'll tell him. I'll tell him. I'll tell him. Tell him. I'll tell him."

"Eh up!" Grandfather called. "You! Charge of the Light Brigade! Balaclava's that road!"

Joseph stopped, breathless.

"Ay," said Grandfather. "I recollect as

how they lost their puff a bit, too. I was cutting bell-cot for the school at the time."

"Grandfather," said Joseph. He was
leaning against the rock of the hill, in the
shade of beeches. "I'll not go with you."

"What?" said Grandfather.

Joseph stood straight. "I'll not cut stone."

"You'll not what?" said Grandfather.

"I can't. You must prentice me to the
smithy."

Grandfather laid his tools down.

"Prentice to the smithy? Prentice to
little Jump James?"

"That's what you must do," said Joseph.
"I've to get me Indentures. I don't want
stone."

"You don't want stone," said Grandfather.

"No."

"And why don't you want stone?"

"Because," said Joseph.

"Because?" said Grandfather. "Because
of what?"

The words blurted out. "Because of you!"

"Oh." Grandfather was still.

"You're all over!" said Joseph. "I must get somewhere: somewhere aback of you. I must. It's my time. Else I'll never."

Grandfather took off his cap and threw it on the road.

"By God!"

He stamped on his cap, and turned around.

"By God!" He stamped again. "Joseph, I thought you'd never speak!"

"Eh?" said Joseph.

"Smithing! By God, that's aback, that is! That's aback of behind!"

"You're not vexed?"

"Vexed? Me?" said Grandfather. "Who'll make the brick-setter's trowel, Joseph? Who'll make the brickie's trowel? Hey!"

His beard danced and he held Joseph at arm's length. "Who-whoop! Wo-whoop! Wo-o-o-o! Who'll make the brickie's trowel? Wo-whoop! Wo-o-o-o!"

Damper Latham came over the crest at

the top of Long Croft field.

Grandfather pulled Joseph with him to the bank. "Act natural," he said. "Give us a thrutch with this." He was lifting a stone into its seat. Joseph eased the ends, and Grandfather tapped the stone sideways with the handle of his hammer. He could have managed it by himself, without help. "There," he said. "She'll do. You'll be able to say we built that one."

"Never think I'm against you," said Joseph. "I've got to carry me own sledge at the forge."

"And you shall," said Grandfather. "Stone and you, you'd never marry: I've seen it, Joseph. And, Joseph, we do us best, but you're a granny reardun, think on, and a granny reardun you'll be. So you get prenticed, and a roof over you, and meat in you, and drink. You're like to have to look to yourself sooner than most in this world. Hey!" he shouted to Damper Latham. "My grandson! See at him! He's going for a generous, ingenious hammerman!"

"He's never!" said Damper Latham. "Woa back!" he said to the horses.

"He is that! Prenticed to little Jump James! What do you think?"

"His Indentures'll need some wetting," said Damper Latham. "Shall I be invited?"

"I'll go see Jump tonight," said Grandfather. "Then it'll be all round the anvil tomorrow and a new barrel from The Bull's Head. Now what've you fetched me?" He looked into the cart. "Gorgeous," he said. "Beautiful. Oh, that's the ticket for soup! Let's be having it."

He unfastened the sides. Joseph tried to help him, but Grandfather wouldn't let him.

"No," he said. "Not my grandson. I'm not having his touch spoilt with raunging."

Damper winked. "Give us a tune, youth," he said, and passed the E-Flat cornet to Joseph.

"You'd best keep her," he said. "She's a good un, but she's an old un, and she'll need looking after now and again to keep her sweet. What do you say, Robert?"

"Oh, he's the only best tinsmith already," said Grandfather. "He'll be learning Jump a thing or two."

Joseph held the cornet, the brass metal.

"You mean it?" he said to Damper Latham.

Damper Latham winked, but differently. There was a sparkle, and he just waved his hand.

Joseph went to the wood and sat in a beech tree root. Grandfather and Damper Latham began to unload the white dimension stone. Joseph sat above them, and played.

The men banged the stones off, and sang.

"Oh, can you wash a soldier's shirt?
And can you wash it clean?
Oh, can you wash a soldier's shirt,
And hang it on the green?"

Joseph played it over and over, faster and faster, descants and triple-tonguing. It was the great song of the Hough, and it never tired.

Damper Latham clapped his cart to, and drove off, beating time still with his curled whip, in the air.

Joseph strode down the wood, loose-legged, and playing, and jigged on the road. He stopped only to polish the shining cornet on the edge of his sleeve; his own cornet, soprano E-Flat.

"Oh, can you wash a soldier's shirt?
*   And can you wash it clean?*
Oh, can you wash a soldier's shirt . . ."

He heard the crake, crake of the broken spring on the bassinet. Mother was coming down the slope of the road by Long Croft field, taking Charlie home for his tea.

". . . And hang it on the green?"

Joseph ran. "See at it! See at it!" he cried. "See at it! Me own! And I'm to be a prenticed smith!"

He always pushed Charlie down Long Croft and under the wood. Charlie liked the speed and rattle of it and the wind in the holes in the bassinet hood.

Joseph set off, full belt, one-handed, playing the cornet with the other. The spring that Grandfather could hold only with rope made the wheels veer to the left. Joseph and Charlie swerved down the hill.

"Oh, can you wash a soldier's shirt?
And can you wash it clean?
Oh, can you wash a soldier's shirt,
And hang it on the green?"

Grandfather took off his cap and whirled it around his head as they passed.

"Who-whoop! Wo-whoop! Wo-o-o-o!"

"Who-whoop! Wo-whoop! Wo-o-o-o!" Joseph answered. The roped spring grated and bounced. Joseph ran on.

"Never mind, Charlie. Wait while I get me sledge. You'll see! I'll mend your bassinet!"

"Who-whoop! Wo-whoop! Wo-o-o-o!"

Charlie laughed. Under the earth, the forge bloomed. Cornet and weathercock, the sun shone, music, turning to the wind.

THE AIMER GATE

THE
AIMER GATE

Robert took Wicked Winnie off the wall and oiled her.

The sky was coming light. It was going to be a hot day, but now it was cold.

Wicked Winnie was made of oak planks and the frame of a bassinet. Robert had mounted a swivel on the front wheels, and fixed a length of sashcord, so that he could steer her.

He went down the path to the road, set

himself, heeled along twice and put his feet on the bar. The wheels were fast on the hill, and Robert had to lean out at the bottom to take the corner into the lane and over the Moss. The Moss was flat, and when the cart stopped, Robert got off and walked, pulling her after him. He reached Faddock Allman's cottage, and knocked.

"Mister Allman!"

"Who goes there?" shouted Faddock Allman. "Friend or foe?"

"Friend," said Robert.

"Advance, Friend, and be recognised!" said Faddock Allman.

The cottage was on a piece of wet land by the road. Robert went in.

Faddock Allman had swept the floor and tidied his bed. His brew can was by him, his cocoa powder and sugar in two twists of paper.

"Have you had breakfast?" said Robert.

"Ay," said Faddock Allman. "Get on parade."

"You'll need your jacket," said Robert. He helped Faddock Allman put it on. There was a ribbon fastened to the jacket with a safety pin, orange, blue and yellow and a medal hung at the end.

Faddock Allman picked up his brew can, dropped the twists of cocoa and sugar inside, fitted the lid, took hold of the handle in his teeth, and swung across the floor on his arms and onto the seat of the cart. He put two sacks by him, one to sit on, one for his shoulders in case it rained, and wedged his brew against the side.

"Reach us me Toby," he said.

The pith helmet Faddock Allman always wore was on the bed. Robert gave it to him. It was high-topped, and covered with khaki cloth. Faddock Allman settled it on his head, eased the chinstrap, and was ready.

Robert passed the sashcord over his neck and under his arms and pulled. Wicked Winnie sank her wheels in the ground, but when she came to the road proper she moved without sticking.

"Retreat! Forward! Charge!" shouted Faddock Allman.

Robert left the Moss and went up the Hough, past his own house, to Leah's Hill.

There were two fields of corn, one above the other, on Leah's Hill. At the hedgeside, by the bottom field, was a space where Faddock Allman sat in summer, breaking stone to make road flints.

Faddock Allman folded the sacks on the ground and swung himself down to them. He rubbed his arms. "By heck, youth," he said, "it's a thin wind aback of Polly Norbury's."

"Must I go fetch you a brew?" said Robert.

"Only if the Missis has put the kettle on," said Faddock Allman. "And get me hammers."

Robert ran with the brew and Wicked Winnie the few yards to home. The kettle was on the fire, and Uncle Charlie was sitting by it, cleaning his rifle.

"Now then, Dick-Richard," he said to Robert.

It was Uncle Charlie's last day of leave. His kitbag and equipment stood smart in a corner. Uncle Charlie was always smart. He shaved morning and night and smelt of soap and had his hair cut every week. He was a lance-corporal in the army and wore a stripe on his sleeve. He was so clean he looked as though he washed with donkey-stone.

But his rifle was cleaner. He cleaned his rifle all the time, rubbing linseed into the wood and fine oil on the metal. Father said Uncle Charlie took his rifle to bed with him.

"Now then, Dick-Richard, what are you at?" said Uncle Charlie.

"Is there a brew for Mister Allman?" said Robert.

"It'll be a bad day when there isn't,"

said Uncle Charlie. "I'll get it."

"I'll fetch his hammers," said Robert.

He ran into the end room of the house. It was full of old things – bolts of dirty silk, tools, grease, iron, nails, screws, grain for the hens and hammers for cutting stone. Father let Faddock Allman use the hammers because they were good for nothing else, but he wouldn't let him have them for his own. They had to come back each night. Father kept everything, even string.

Uncle Charlie had put the cocoa and sugar on the table and filled the brew can with tea.

"Come on, Dick-Richard," he said. "Let's be having you."

He slung his rifle on his shoulder, picked up the brew can and went out. Robert ran after him with Wicked Winnie and the hammers.

Men and women were gathering at Leah's Hill. Ozzie Leah had brought a load for the day; scythes, whetstones, bantspinners, rakes, food and drink. The fields were too steep for the self-binder to reap on. He was going to have the corn cut by hand. And the only men skilled to scythe together in a team were Ozzie and Young Ollie Leah and Uncle Charlie.

Robert had never seen Leah's Hill sown. It was always pasture. But, with the war, even the rough meadows were ploughed now.

"Eh up, Starie Chelevek," Uncle Charlie said to Faddock Allman. "Here's your brew." He poured tea out of the can, using the lid as a cup.

Faddock Allman shuffled round on his sack and took the cup. He drank, sucked his lips and held out the lid for more. "That's the ticket," he said.

"Mark time on this," said Uncle Charlie, "and then we'll see if we can't fetch you a drop of Ozzie's stagger-juice."

Faddock Allman laughed.

"And cop hold of this for us," said Uncle

Charlie. He rattled the bolt of his rifle, opened it, checked that the breech was empty, took off the magazine, put the gun together again and handed it to Faddock Allman.

Faddock Allman shouldered the rifle, saluted, and put it down on the sacking and covered it against dust.

"All in!" shouted Ozzie Leah.

The three men took their scythes and a whetstone each and sharpened the blades, two strokes below the edge, one above. The metal rang like swords and bells.

"Here's your hammers, Mister Allman," said Robert.

"Wait on," said Faddock Allman. "I've not finished me brew."

The men stood in a line, at the field edge, facing the hill, Ozzie on the outside, and began their swing. It was a slow swing, scythes and men like a big clock, back and to, back and to, against the hill they walked. They walked and swung, hips forward, letting the weight cut. It was as if they were walking in a yellow water before them. Each blade came up in time with each blade, at Ozzie's march, for if they ever got out of time the blades would cut flesh and bone.

Behind each man the corn swarf lay like silk in the light of poppies. And the women gathered the swarf by armfuls, spun bants of straw and tied in armfuls into sheaves, stacked sheaves into kivvers. Six sheaves stood to a kivver, and the kivvers must stand till the church bells had rung over them three times. Three weeks to harvest: but first was the getting.

Faddock Allman had finished his brew and was sitting, his hands on his leg stumps, watching the men cut the hill.

"You'll be wanting stones, Mister All-man," said Robert.

"Wait on, wait on," said Faddock Allman.

The three men reached the corner by the

gate to the top field, and pivoted in rhythm on the inside man, Young Ollie Leah. Their line was as straight as soldiers, and when Ozzie was abreast they moved forward along the hill.

"Gorgeous," said Faddock Allman.

"Whet!" shouted Ozzie at the end of a blade swing, and the men stopped and sharpened up, two strokes below, one above; two and one, two and one, like a tune. And then they put the whetstones back in their pockets and began to cut again.

"Right, youth," said Faddock Allman. "I've been waiting to get at that devil all year."

"What?" said Robert.

"Yonder," said Faddock Allman.

"Where?" said Robert.

"Go up past them kivvers," said Faddock Allman, "and just inside top field, against the corn, you'll see a little jackacre of land, by itself."

"I know," said Robert.

"Ay, well, if you have a good feckazing in there, you'll see the best stone for road flints there is in the Hough."

"Right, Mister Allman," said Robert, and pulled Wicked Winnie round into the field and up the hill. The ground between the kivvers was sharp stubble that put a polish on his boot soles. He kept slipping, and the stubble caught his knees.

He reached the gate between the two fields. And beyond it there was a dip and a hump of green, with nettles and a few thistles going to seed. The patch was a bite out of the crop.

Robert opened the gate and went in. The rough pasture hadn't been ploughed and the meadow grass was thick. He could feel hardness ruckled under the ground, but he couldn't reach it.

He chopped with the edge of his heel irons at the biggest lump. He kept kicking. The grass came away in tufts, not strong enough to peel, but snagged with white roots. Robert chopped the roots until he reached sand. In the sand there was a corner of stone. He pulled at it but it didn't move. He stamped on it but it didn't break. He got his hand to it, and wrenched. The stone raggled like a tooth, enough to show between it and its own shape in the ground.

Robert tried to lift it straight out, but his hands wouldn't grip and he fell over. He knelt and scooped the sandy earth away, digging along the stone.

It was a proper stone, worked and dressed, and he had hold of one corner. The sides went away from the squared corner and there was nothing for him to grip. The stone went back into the hill.

Robert tugged sideways again. More space showed, and he felt the stone move. He scooped more sand. The stone was yellow white. Now it wagged but wouldn't come. He felt each swing jolt, and had to stop for breath. The grip was going from his fingers; so he spat on his hands, rubbed them together and tugged straight.

The stone sighed out, and he held it. It was a stone clear as a brick, but bigger.

"What the heck?" said Robert.

Now that the hill was open he could reach inside. There was more stone, all the same yellow white, a lot of it cob-ends of rubble, but every piece true. They came more easily the more he got. If a big piece stuck he took the smaller pieces from around and beneath it. Wicked Winnie was soon filled and she was a weight.

Robert held her at full stretch of the sashcord, using himself as a brake, and let her down the hill to Faddock Allman.

"Whet!" shouted Ozzie.

Every step jarred, and he had to stab at the ground with his heels to hold Wicked Winnie from running away with him. He went down the cleared ground of the swarfs.

Then he slipped. The stubble was too polished. Robert sat down hard and slid.

Wicked Winnie was trying to pull him forwards, but he lay back, holding the sashcord, lay back, pressing his shoulders
against the hill, his heels furrowing. He
didn't want to be dragged face down through
that stubble.

Kivvers were all about him. Robert
heaved at the sashcord and rolled his body
to steer. And Wicked Winnie swung close
but didn't hit. The last kivver went by, and
Robert, Wicked Winnie and the stones all
landed in the quickthorn hedge.

"Yon's a grand lot," said Faddock
Allman.

"Whet!" shouted Ozzie.

Up and down the field Robert went. He
had never had such a day. When he got
stones for Faddock Allman he had to find
them one by one, all sorts, in lanes and
hedge cops and at the ends of fields, every
kind and size. Now, though, it seemed the
hill was giving them to him.

"Is that enough, Mister Allman?" said

Robert. He had made a pile that would last till winter.

"Is it heck as like!" said Faddock Allman. "Raunge the beggars out!" So Robert did.

And the scythes went round the field, cutting a square spiral to the centre. The rows of kivvers grew under the heat of the day.

"Baggin!" shouted Ozzie Leah.

The field stopped. Men and women went to the shaded edge, where food and beer were kept. The scythes were sharpened and laid against trees.

"Eh up, Starie Chelevek! Fancy a wet?" Uncle Charlie had left the others and come down to be with Faddock Allman. He'd brought baggin of bread and onion and cheese and a stone bottle of beer, a full gallon. He crouched on one heel and swigged from the bottle. "And what have you been at, Dick-Richard," he said, "mauling guts out of jackacres?"

"It's all cut stone," said Robert, "same as a quarry bank!"

"It is that," said Faddock Allman. He took the bottle from Uncle Charlie and drank. "See at it!" He hit a finished, squared perfect block and it broke into rough road flints. "Grand," said Faddock Allman.

"What's it doing there?" said Robert.

"Nowt," said Faddock Allman. "Grand!" He split another.

"Are all jackacres cut stone?" said Robert.

"Happen," said Faddock Allman. "Number One! Fire!" He smashed a stone. "Number Two! Fire!" He smashed another.

Uncle Charlie uncovered his rifle and polished the stock. He smiled.

"Number Three!" shouted Faddock Allman.

"Cease firing and get your baggin," said Uncle Charlie.

"Cease firing! Scatter homeward!" shouted Faddock Allman, and bit into an onion, and chewed. He laughed at Robert.

"I was twitting you, youth," he said. "You see, I recollect as how, at one time of day, there was a house stood yonder. And I recollect as how, when they fetched it down, I did enjoy chucking cob-ends through windows."

"All in!" shouted Ozzie.

"It was good," said Faddock Allman, "chucking cob-ends." He pulled the peak of his helmet over his eyes. "Number Three! Fire! Number Four! Fire!" He laughed at the rock.

Robert emptied Wicked Winnie, and went to take Father his baggin.

Father was a smith. He was tinsmith, locksmith and blacksmith: and every Monday morning he wound the chapel clock. But now his time went on making horse-shoes for the war.

Robert swept Wicked Winnie clean and

oiled her again. He oiled the hubs specially, with Uncle Charlie's fine oil.

He set her in the middle of the road, at the top of the camber, and eased himself in, holding the sashcord. Wicked Winnie wanted to go, but Robert put his boots down. He took his balance, waited for stillness, and gently lifted his boots, not pushing. Nothing happened. He tried not to twitch. Then Wicked Winnie began to move. Robert sat in a crouch, and steered.

The first part of the road was steep and easy, and Wicked Winnie went fast. At the bottom of the hill the road turned upwards and then down again past Long Croft field and under the wood to Chorley. Robert kept to the top of the camber, crouched as small as Faddock Allman.

At the other end of the wood the road ran to a crest that was so low and long that it could be felt more than seen. This was the worst part. Wicked Winnie lost all her speed, coasted, crept, and reached the top.

And at the top she always stopped. But today there was no wind. Robert had taken Uncle Charlie's fine oil to the hubs, the very best. She was still going. Another yard was all she needed.

Wicked Winnie crept. Her wheels were turning. Robert held his breath. His chest was tight. His tongue stuck to his teeth. But he wouldn't breathe.

His eyes started to see rainbows and his head buzzed. Rainbows round everything; boots, wheels, spokes, hubs. The hubs were still. He looked at the rims. They moved, just moved. There was a noise in his ears like a brook. But he didn't breathe. The hard tyres had flecks on them from the road, and the flecks were still moving. They were moving. They were moving faster. Robert let in a sip of air. Wicked Winnie didn't stop. Robert breathed.

Uncle Charlie's oil had done it.

Now it was a straight run to the smithy: a measured mile from home to the smithy, and Wicked Winnie had broken her record, with Uncle Charlie's oil.

"She did it!" Robert shouted, and sat up. "She did it, she did it, she did it!"

Wicked Winnie rolled along under the chapel clock and across the main road to the smithy and lodged against the kerb. Robert ran into the smithy with Father's baggin.

It was noise at the forge, dark and red. The men were making horseshoes, and the apprentice worked the bellows. It was cutting and snapping, heating, sledging, twisting and breaking. Father wasn't there.

Robert ran out again. He pulled Wicked Winnie behind him, swirling her track in patterns in the dust. He hitched her to the chapel gate and went in. He opened the tower door.

The clock struck ten. Robert knew where Father was. Every day, at ten o'clock, the time was sent from London along the telegraph wires, and the signalman opened the window of the signalbox and rang the shining bell that hung outside. And each Monday, Father went to the railway bridge and stood with his fob watch in his hand to check the time, and when the bell rang he set his watch to ten o'clock and walked down the village to the chapel to set the clock.

He was on the bridge now, waiting for that brass bell. If it rang a lot sooner or a lot later than the chapel, Father would be vexed all day. He had looked after the clock ever since he had finished being an apprentice.

The station bell rang. The clock was fast, but not much.

Robert dragged a thick square of coconut matting across the tiles and put it in the middle of the floor. There was an extending ladder hanging on the wall in the corner. Father would lift it and swing it in one move down to the mat, and push the extension up to the high platform under the roof of the first bay of the tower. Robert had often seen him do it. It was easy.

Robert took hold of the rungs, and lifted straight upwards. The ladder was heavy, but it came off its hook. Robert turned to put the ladder on the mat, but the ladder kept on turning, and took Robert with it and fell back against the wall, next to its hook. It was too heavy to lift and too heavy to put down. Robert was stuck. He turned again, and stopped as soon as the ladder moved. The ladder turned past him, but he was able to drop the end on the mat, so that it wouldn't skid.

Now Robert had the ladder in the middle of the tower, upright, wobbling, but it couldn't reach the high platform without its extension. The extension slid over the bottom half of the ladder and its own weight on hooks kept it clamped to the rungs.

Robert got his shoulder to the ladder, his legs either side of it, and lifted the extension off its first rung. The extension slid upwards, past two more rungs. Robert's grip trembled. The ladder began to lean, and with its leaning it was heavier all at once, too heavy, and the hooks were between rungs and he couldn't lock them. The ladder fell away from him, and the extension bent like a stalk.

Robert was losing his strength, as he had with the jackacre stone on the hill.

He bent and pushed again, and stuck. He felt as though he had no muscles, only a hot sharp ache, and a sharp sweet taste in his mouth. He let the hooks down on the rung. The ladder was safe; firm against the matting. It wouldn't skid. The top of the ladder was at the high platform.

Robert held the baggin cloth between his teeth, and climbed. It was a whippy ladder and it bounced under him.

From the platform there was a fixed set of steps, with iron handrails, to a trapdoor in the ceiling. The trap was lashed to a tread. Robert undid the lashing and pushed

with his fingers. The trap opened, as if
somebody was in the bay above, lifting. But
the door had been counterweighted by
Father with sashcord and bricks.

Robert went into the second bay of the
tower.

Here the clock did not tick. From the
road, the gentle noise could be heard, but
in the second bay the pendulum swung its
arc, and the clock spoke. It spoke with the
same beat, but no whispered tick. The
whole dark bay was the sound. Sunlight
criss-crossed the floor through stained glass
with marks like coloured chalks, and the
air above thudded the pendulum.

A twenty-nine stave ladder led to the
clock chamber above. The ladder had its
own rhythm, no whip or bend, no clattering
extension.

Robert always stopped to watch when he
was on the ladder. The pendulum came and
went in the dim light, came and went.
Through the trapdoor and past the plat-

form the floor tiles were a long way off.

He climbed up, stepped sideways from the ladder to the planks of the chamber and put the baggin against the clock.

Here, everything was different again, and open. The clock case was like a hen coop, covered with tarred felt, and out of holes in the roof and sides rods connected the gears of its four faces, wires ran over pulleys to the weights that drove the clock, and a chain held the striker of the bell.

The slanted louvres filled each wall, and Robert could see the village, across to the station and Saint Philip's church. Saint Philip's had a gilded weathercock, but nothing that could tell the time. The wind and hours in Chorley were at different ends.

Robert watched the hands move on the faces of the clock. The faces held white glass in metal frames, and Father had made the hands. From inside the chamber the time was back to front.

Robert wedged himself up the wall and

reached for the cross-beam that held the frame of the clock. He hung, pulled, swung one leg over, then the other, and sat on top of the beam. He squirmed along the beam, close under the chamber roof. There was a small hatch in the roof, without hinges. He pushed at it, and it lifted and dropped back hard. It was heavy for a small square of wood. He tried again, lifting with his shoulders, and the hatch opened enough for him to jam his elbow through, then his arm, and to work the hatch sideways and clear.

Above him was darkness. But it wasn't quiet. He listened to the sound. It was no sound of clocks or of anything made. It was as if the wind had a voice and was flying in the steeple. The sound moved, never still, and under the sound was a high roaring.

Robert lifted himself on his arms through the hatchway, his legs clear of the beam. He rolled backwards and was in. He lifted the hatch, biting his lip with the heaviness, and settled it in its place. He moved gently over the floor to the wall of the steeple and sat down, hugging his knees.

The floor was smooth, covered with lead. There was lead on the hatch, and that was the weight. Robert sat in the darkness and listened to the voices above him.

It was his special place. No one else came here, to the lead-floored room in the pinnacle. No one else heard the sound.

He sat and waited for the sweeping in the air to clear. It softened, was quiet, then still. It was not all dark in the steeple. There were holes, crockets of decoration on the spire, and through them came enough light for him to see.

The room rose to a point far above, to the very capstone, and an iron bar came down through the capstone to a short beam that spanned the walls, and the bar was bolted through the beam.

A ladder went up to the beam. And on the ladder, the beam and every rough stone and brick end there were pigeons. They had flown when the hatch moved, but now the last of them was settling back, or hovering under the crockets. That had been the sound.

Beam, ladder and floor were white with droppings. It was Robert's secret cave in the air, which only pigeons knew. But the soft floor was covered with footprints, shoes and clogs and boots of every size, covered and filled with droppings, as though all the children from the village and the Moss and the Hough played here. But Robert was every one. It had been his room and place for years, and nobody knew.

Robert stood up. "Cush-cush," he said. "Cush-a-cush." The pigeons watched him, but didn't fly. He took a step on the floor, and paused, another, to the ladder. He put his hand out for a rung. A pigeon dabbed at him with its beak, but he didn't flinch. "Cush-cush." He took hold of another rung and set his weight on the ladder. "Cush-

cush. Cush-a-cush." A pigeon fluttered, and above him he heard others go. He held still until they were still. Then he began again.

In the high cave of the pinnacle Robert climbed the ladder of birds. Sometimes their voices and wings would swirl, brushing him, making shadows in shadows, and he would stop until the ladder was quiet again. Then he would climb, careful with feet and hands to ease between the birds. And the birds made space for him.

The wall closed. He could see every facet of the spire tapering around. Through the crockets there were small pictures of land. He climbed.

Robert came to the beam. From the ladder he grasped the capstone iron and stepped onto the beam. It was slippery with droppings. Below him the white ladder rustled.

"Cush-cush. Cush-a-cush," said Robert.

He looked up into the black point. Some

of the stone showed. He stretched, and reached on tip-toe to see if he had grown. He hadn't. The iron bar was long.

In all his secret, the capstone was the only part that Robert couldn't reach.

He felt the bar. It was rusty, but not sharp. And it was thick. Robert spat on his hands and took hold. He hitched himself off the beam, drew his knees up and gripped the bar with his feet. The rust held him. He stretched hand over hand, brought up his feet, gripped, hand over hand, feet; gripped. He was there. His head fitted under the capstone and his shoulders filled the spire.

Robert looked down at the birds.

The inside of the spire was rough. He put out one hand and found a hold to push against. He found another. He pressed his head to the capstone. He was firm.

Arms out, head up, Robert uncrossed his feet and let them hang. He was wearing the steeple. It fitted like a hat. He was wearing the steeple all the way to the earth, a stone dunce's cap.

> *"Dunce, dunce, double-D,*
> *Can't learn his ABC!"*

Robert sang, and waved his legs.

The ladder fluttered. He stopped. He took hold of the bar, and found nooks for his feet. There was nothing else.

There was nothing else. His own and private place was only this, and he felt it leave him. In all the years, there had been the last part waiting. Now he was there, and he was alone all at once, high above beam, birds, clock and no more secrets.

Robert scratched the stone with his finger. He picked at mortar and it fell. Some birds went out through the crockets. He put the flat of his hand on the top course, banged it: and stopped. He couldn't see, but his hand could feel. There was a mark on the stone, cut deep. His fingers fitted. It was a mark like an arrow. He tried to see, but there wasn't enough light.

Robert nudged his head to be more comfortable against the capstone, and felt again. It was an arrow cut into stone dressed smooth as Faddock Allman's jack-acre rocks. Robert's hand was against his face, and he walked his fingers along the course.

Right at the top of the spire, where no one could tell, the stone had been worked. Something had mattered. There was no rough rag, patched with brick. The stone was true though it would never be seen.

Robert's fingers touched a mark. It was cut as deep as the arrow, but was straight and round lines together. It was writing. Real writing. And Robert shouted so that all the birds winged and filled the steeple and beat around him. His hands were reading over and over the carved letters, over and over they read his own name.

Robert slid down the bar to beam and ladder, clattered down among buffeting wings and fear. He took no care. The droppings were slime.

He jumped his own height from the ladder

to the floor and shoved the hatch open, fell through to the cross-beam of the clock, rolled, hung, let go and landed on the edge of the platform.

"By heck!" Father had been oiling the clock, but he banged the case shut against the dust and feathers that came down with Robert. "What are you at?"

Robert ran round to the other side of the clock.

"And what have you been rolling in?" said Father. "Your mother'll play the dickens. By heck! Don't come no nearer. We could take a nest of wasps with you!"

"There's been someone up there," said Robert.

"Never," said Father. "Only you's daft enough."

"And they've carved me name," said Robert. "My name! Me own full name. Why?"

"Where's this?" said Father.

"Up top," said Robert. "Right under

the capstone."

"What do you mean, 'your' name?" said Father.

"Me name. My name. Spelt proper," said Robert.

"Oh," said Father. "And I'll lay you a wager it was beautifully done, too."

"I felt it," said Robert. "My name."

"And every inch of stone smooth as butter," said Father. "By God, ay."

"Was it you?" said Robert.

"Me?" said Father. "No, youth. That must've been cut fifty-three years or more."

"But me name!" said Robert.

"It's not your name," said Father. "It's my grandfather's. Ay. Old Robert. He was a proud, bazzil-arsed devil. But he was a good un."

Robert came from behind the clock. Father sat down on his heel and opened the baggin.

"I knew he'd capped the steeple, same as he did at Saint Philip's. But I didn't ever know him to put his name to anything. His mark, yes: never his name. Happen it mattered."

"There was a mark," said Robert. "An arrow."

"That's him," said Father. "Now you'll see his mark all over. But you have to look. He was a beggar, and he did like to tease. Well, well."

"And am I called after him?" said Robert.

"Ay, but not to much purpose yet, seemingly," said Father. He ate an onion.

"He was everywhere, all over," said Father. "But I got aback of him. A smith's aback of everyone, you see. You can't make nothing without you've a smith for your tools. But I don't know what there is for you to get aback of, youth."

"I'm going up top again," said Robert.

"Well, see as you close that hatch," said Father. "I want no feathers in me baggin, nor in the clock, neither."

Robert climbed back into the pinnacle, and closed the hatch. The birds had nearly all left the steeple in fright. A few fluttered, no longer knowing him.

His secret room for years. And, at the top, a secret. Robert took hold of the ladder.

He reached the beam, the bar, and up. When his head touched the capstone he found good bracing for his feet, and let his hands lie on the top course of stone.

In the dark his hands could read. And in the dark his hands could hear. There was a long sound in the stone. It was no sound unless Robert heard it, and meant nothing unless he gave it meaning. His chosen place had chosen him. Its end was the beginning.

Robert went down, slowly. He was gentle with the hatch. Father had the clock open and was oiling it.

"That's put a quietness on you," he said.

"Ay."

"What is it most?" said Father.

"He knew it wouldn't be seen," said

Robert. "But he did it good as any."

"Ay," said Father.

The clock hung in an iron frame. It was all rods cogs and wheels. It kept time twice. There was a drive to the hours and minutes and the pendulum, and a drive to the bell hammer. The bell was fixed, and the hour was struck on it. Both drives were weights held by two cables, each wound to a drum. The weights fitted in slots that ran down to the base of the tower.

Every week Father cleaned and oiled the clock, and wound the weights back up. It took them a week to drop the height of the tower. He wound the cables with a key like a crank handle.

"She's getting two minutes," said Father. "It's this dry weather." He reached into the clock, among the wheels and cogs and the governor that kept all steady, and he turned a small brass plate to the right. The plate was the top of the pendulum sweeping the bay below. "Just a toucher," said Father.

He did it by feel. The rhythm of the pendulum sounded the same, but Father had made it swing a little further, a little longer, and the clock would slow to the right time, until the weather changed.

"Give us a pound on the windlass, youth," said Father.

Robert liked this part of the job. It was better than turning the mangle at home, lumpy and wet.

The drums took up the cable.

"What makes wheels go round?" said Robert.

Father looked at him from the other side of the clock, through the cogs and gears.

"You, you swedgel," said Father.

"I mean wheels," said Robert. "What makes them turn?"

"You shove them," said Father.

"But why do they go round?" said Robert.

"Come here," said Father. "This side."

Robert left the winding.

"Now see at these; these wheels here," said Father. "All different sorts and sizes, aren't they, and all act according to each other?"

"Ay," said Robert.

"And if that little un there should stop, so would that big un yonder. It's all according, do you see?"

"Ay."

"Well, now," said Father, "have you ever asked yourself what makes this clock go? Have you the foggiest idea?"

Robert shook his head.

"It's this wheel," said Father. "It's the escapement."

In the middle of the clock there was a brass wheel, with pegs set on the rim of the face. Two iron teeth rocked in and out from either side by turns, holding and releasing the pegs, and the wheel came round. The teeth on the pegs were the tick of the clock.

"You wouldn't think so small a thing could make so great a sound," said Father.

"But that's escapement. And the tick goes into the pendulum. You couldn't have time without you had escapement."

"Could you not?" said Robert.

"That weight you're winding must try to get back to the ground, mustn't it?" said Father. "So it's pulling on that cable. And the cable turns the wheels. But them teeth, see at them. That comes in and catches the peg, and stops the wheel, stops the whole clock: but the pendulum's swinging, see, and in comes the other and pushes the peg forwards, and out pops the other tooth, and the pendulum swings, and back comes the tooth. Stop. Start. Day and night, for evermore: regular. It's the escapement."

"I only asked why wheels go round," said Robert.

"And I'm telling you. It's escapement," said Father. "Why do you think them weights drop at all? You could say as you weren't winding weights up, you were winding chapel down. It comes to the same. It's all according, gears and cogs. We're going at that much of a rattle, the whole blooming earth, moon and stars, we need escapement to hold us together."

"I must go help me Uncle Charlie," said Robert, and stepped onto the ladder, into the pendulum bay.

"That's right," said Father. "I knew I could've saved me breath."

Robert went.

"By, it's a day's work to watch you put the kettle on," said Father.

Robert went.

"Hey!" Father called after him.

"What?" said Robert.

"Was it you as took the extension off the wall and reared it up?"

"Ay!"

"By yourself?"

"Ay!"

"You're shaping, youth," said Father.

Robert untied Wicked Winnie, and ran with her along the road. "What's he on at?"

he said. " 'Escapement'? That's not escape-ment. It's fine oil."

He was able to ride a little under the wood, but he had to keep running to push.

"Who-whoop! Wo-whoop! Wo-o-o-o!"

Robert heard the distant cry of the summer fields go up on Leah's Hill.

"Who-whoop! Wo-whoop! Wo-o-o-o!"

The men were excited. "Who-whoop! Wo-whoop! Wo-o-o-o! Who-whoop! Wo-whoop! Wo-o-o-o!"

Then Robert heard a shot. It was hard, not like a gun. There was another. And four quickly after that. And silence. Robert listened. There was no sound. The heat was pressing the day flat, and the air thick with it.

Robert left Wicked Winnie at the gate and ran into the house. He could hear Mother making the beds.

"Father's fettling the clock!" he called up the bent stairs. "I'm off up Leah's!"

But first Robert cleaned Wicked Winnie

again, and rubbed linseed into her wood. Then he put the kettle on the fire for Faddock Allman's brew, and went out.

The bottom field was cut, neat with kivvers. The men and women were eating their food under the hedge. Uncle Charlie was leaving for the road. He had his rifle slung on one shoulder and Faddock Allman over the other.

"Dick-Richard! I want you!" he shouted.

"What for?" said Robert.

"Never mind what for. Let's be having you. The tooter the sweeter."

Robert ran to where Uncle Charlie stood by the gate.

"Gently does it, Starie Chelevek," said Uncle Charlie. And he carefully set Faddock Allman down in Wicked Winnie.

"Where's he going?" said Robert.

"He's having his dinner with me," said Uncle Charlie.

"At our house?" said Robert.

"Where else?" said Uncle Charlie.

"Has Father said?"

"He's not been asked," said Uncle Charlie. He bent down to Faddock Allman's helmet. It had slipped over one ear.

"I'll have me brew same as usual," said Faddock Allman. "Young un fetches for me."

"Eyes front," said Uncle Charlie. "Straighten your pith pot. Get on parade, me old Toby."

"Was that you shooting?" said Robert.

"Ay," said Uncle Charlie. "I'm back at work Tuesday: so I might as good practise."

"I'll not come in," said Faddock Allman. "I'll not disturb your dinners."

They had reached the house.

"Who's having their dinners disturbed?" said Uncle Charlie.

"I'd sooner not," said Faddock Allman.

"What must I do?" said Robert.

"Bung him round the back," said Uncle Charlie. "He can sun hisself, and I'll feed him through the window."

Robert took Faddock Allman round the side of the house and put him against the white limewash, under the thatch.

"Shan't you be too hot, Mister Allman?" said Robert.

"Champion," said Faddock Allman. "Grand." He watched the sun.

Robert went back in.

"Will he be all right?" he said. "It's a whole topcoat warmer against our back wall."

"Not for that old sweat," said Uncle Charlie. "He did his soldiering in Mesopolonica. He's used to it."

Uncle Charlie lifted the boiling kettle off the fire and made a brew of cocoa. He took the brew, the kettle and his rifle with him into the garden.

"Warm enough?" he said.

"Grand," said Faddock Allman.

Uncle Charlie gave him his brew. Then he cleaned his rifle. He put the bolt and the magazine on one side and poured the boiling water down the barrel, the whole five pint kettle.

He looked into the barrel from both ends, and pulled a length of rag through, fastened to a cord, time and time again until the rifle was dry. He picked up his oil bottle; and frowned.

"Who's had this?" he said. "Some beggar's touched this."

"It was me," said Robert.

"And who gave you permission?" said Uncle Charlie.

"It wasn't more than a drop," said Robert. "I needed it for her wheels."

"I don't care what you need," said Uncle Charlie. "And you don't touch, think on."

He oiled the moving parts of the gun, the catches, magazine, levers, bolt and barrel.

Father came round the corner of the house. He had put his bicycle against the gable end. He stopped when he saw Faddock Allman.

"Now then, Faddock," said Father.

"Now then, Joseph," said Uncle Charlie.

Faddock Allman drank his brew and said nothing. Father looked at Uncle Charlie and went inside.

"Put the kettle on, Dick-Richard," said Uncle Charlie.

Robert filled the kettle, and took it to the fire. Mother was serving Father his dinner. Robert ran back again quickly.

Uncle Charlie had assembled his rifle and was rattling the breech open and closed.

"Ease! Springs!" shouted Faddock Allman.

Father shut the window from inside.

Uncle Charlie smiled. "We're a right pair, aren't we, Dick-Richard? Your father and me? Him sitting up in that chapel, like a great barn owl, oiling his clock. And me, oiling this. Eh?"

Robert pointed to a bent piece of metal on the rifle. "Is that the escapement?" he said.

"The eswhatment?" said Uncle Charlie.

"That's the cocking piece locking re-
sistence."

"Oh," said Robert.

"I'd best be doing," said Faddock
Allman. "Now as Master's having his
dinner."

"You stand easy, Starie Chelevek," said
Uncle Charlie. "I'll fetch you some dinner
meself."

"No. I'll be off. Young un takes me,"
said Faddock Allman.

"Does he?" said Uncle Charlie. He
picked up Wicked Winnie's sashcord and
put two turns of it around the boot scraper
by the door and pulled all his weight on the
knot. "Let him unfasten that, then. Come
on, Dick-Richard. There's top field to be
cut this after."

He took his rifle and Robert into the
house and sat at the table, on the sofa by
the window. Father was eating. Robert
stood near the door. Mother poured fresh
tea.

"It's not brewed," said Father.

"It's wet," said Uncle Charlie.

"Why isn't this tea brewed?" said Father.

"By, it's close in here, isn't it, Joseph?" said Uncle Charlie, and opened the window. Father leaned across and shut it.

"Give over," said Uncle Charlie. "I've been second man to Ozzie Leah on the scythe all morning, and I could do with a drop of coolth."

Father tapped the table with his square-ended fingers as he spoke. "What's yon Mossaggot think he's doing here while I'm having me dinner?" he said.

"I fetched him. I'm feeding him," said Uncle Charlie.

"There's a war on," said Father.

"Eh up! Where?" said Uncle Charlie. "Now, Joseph: Charlie's home. Joseph, whenever has the stockpot gone short when Charlie's home, eh? There's good flesh-meat, isn't there, and without granching

your teeth on lead shot? Come on, Joseph.
Charlie's home."

He put his hand on Father's arm. His own
arm was thin and brown under the golden
hairs. Father looked down at the arm.

"Get off with your mithering," said
Father. He ate angrily.

"I seem to recollect, Joseph," said Uncle
Charlie, "as how it hadn't used to matter so
much when Faddock Allman was being
shot to beggary by them Boers."

Father didn't answer. Uncle Charlie cut
a round of bread, spread it with dripping,
and opened the window. "Cop hold," he
said to Faddock Allman, and left the window
open.

"Eh, Dick-Richard," said Uncle Charlie.
"Your father's vexed, seemingly. What
must we do to cheer him up?"

Robert looked quickly at Father, and
caught a flash of blue eye. Robert said
nothing.

"Here, Dick-Richard," said Uncle
Charlie. "Over here."

Robert went. Father ate. Robert was ready to run.

But Uncle Charlie was quicker. He grabbed Robert with both hands, and lifted him and stood him on the table. Robert's boots clattered among the dishes and his head touched the ceiling beams. He was looking into both men's eyes.

"Give us a song, Dick-Richard," said Uncle Charlie. "One for to win a war with, eh? A penny. See." He pulled a penny out of his pocket and slid it on the table, holding it under his finger. Robert looked at Father again, but Father was eating.

Robert's boots shuffled the tea pot. He felt Uncle Charlie's hand firm holding to his britches. So he sang.

> *"Kitchener's Army,*
> *Working all day,*
> *What does he pay them?*
> *A shilling a day.*
> *What if they grumble?*
> *The Colonel will say,*

> *'Put them in the guardroom,*
> *And stop all their pay'."*

Uncle Charlie hefted Robert down by his britches, and pushed the penny towards him.

Robert took the penny. Father still ate.

"Dear, dear, Joseph," said Uncle Charlie. "Will music never sooth the savage breast? What else can we do?"

He took the bolt and magazine out of his rifle, squinted down the barrel, and put it to his lips as if it were a trumpet. He blew a note.

"Just tuning," said Uncle Charlie. "No harm done."

He blew again, and, by altering the shape of his lips, he played the notes of "Abide With Me". His face was dark red and his eyes rolled.

"You daft ha'porth!" Father nearly choked on his food. Uncle Charlie tried to wink at Robert, and went on playing. "You

lommering, gawming, kay-pawed gowf!"
shouted Father, and coughed and laughed
his dinner over the table. "Give over! Any
allsorts can play that dirge! Let's have some
triple-tonguing!"

"What tune must I play?" said Uncle
Charlie.

"There's not but one tune," said Father.
He opened the corner cupboard and took
out his own E Flat cornet. "There's not but
one tune." He wet his lips, loosened the
valves of the cornet, and looked at Robert.
"I'll give you the note, youth. But you can
stay off the table. Right!"

Father and Uncle Charlie drew in breath
together, and Father began the great tune of
the Hough, triple-tongued, fast. Uncle
Charlie hit what notes he could, and Robert
sang to the soprano E Flat.

"Oh, can you wash a soldier's shirt?
And can you wash it clean?
Oh, can you wash a soldier's shirt,
And hang it on the green?"

"And again!" shouted Father. "Ready!"

"Retreat! Forward! Charge!" shouted Faddock Allman beneath the window.

Robert couldn't sing. His neck hurt. Uncle Charlie slid under the table with laughing. And Father played, his cap on his head, standing above his dinner, and played until the tune was finished.

"Ay," said Father. "Mesopolonica."

After dinner, Robert took Faddock Allman back to the stones by the roadside. Uncle Charlie walked with him, carrying his rifle and a spade from the end room of the house.

"Your father," said Uncle Charlie. "Take no notice. He was a bit upset."

"I know," said Robert.

"He's a man very fluent in giving."

"I know."

"It's them horseshoes and the hours," said Uncle Charlie. "They could take his touch away for ever, him as is the only best smith from Chorley to Mottram. If I was Joseph, I reckon I'd live in chapel clock till this lot was done with. But I'm lucky, Dick-Richard. It's me trade. Now. What shall you be?"

Uncle Charlie lifted Faddock Allman onto his sacking and gave him the hammers, and the rifle.

"I've not thought," said Robert.

"Well, what do you want?"

"All in!" shouted Ozzie Leah.

The men and women moved to the top field.

"What do you want?" Uncle Charlie said again.

Robert went with him, pulling Wicked Winnie, up the hill towards the jackacre patch.

"I like seeing to Mister Allman," said Robert. "And getting for him."

"Good God, youth, that's no trade!" said Uncle Charlie. "You want craft and masterness in you! You're no Mossaggot! You're a Houghite! You must have a trade!"

"Can I work with you, then?" said Robert.

Uncle Charlie picked up his scythe and gave the spade to Robert.

"I work by meself," he said. "I've no apprentices."

"Have you not?" said Robert.

"No, I haven't," said Uncle Charlie.

"I can be a soldier if I want," said Robert.

"And why do you want?" said Uncle Charlie.

"The marching and that," said Robert. "And they give you medals, same as you and Mister Allman."

"Your father calls them bits stuck on the outside of one chap for sticking bits on the inside of another," said Uncle Charlie. "And he's right. No, youth. You must have the flavour for soldiering. I've got it, and you haven't. It's not in you. Now then: here's your next fatigue."

They were at the jackacre patch. It was a

sandhole with stones, ragged at the edge
from Robert's morning.

"You can fill this lot in," said Uncle
Charlie, "and grass it over."

"I'll not fill that in!" said Robert.
"There's ever so many stones come out."

"No," said Uncle Charlie, "but you can
smooth it round for Ozzie Leah to lead his
cart in for the kivvers when they've stood.
He'd break an axle, the way you've got it
now."

Ozzie Leah, Uncle Charlie and Young
Ollie took their stand in the field. The
scythes lifted and the swarfs fell. Round the
field they went. The sun shone.

Robert tried to level the hole. It was a
lonely, hot job, dull, not like the morning
when everything was being found. He
shovelled and sweated, patched the ground
with turf and trod it in.

The sun was so hot that it took all colour
from the land.

"Whet!" shouted Ozzie.

Everywhere but the corn was black and dark green. Saint Philip's church was black, its weathervane cockerel black and just proud of the horizon. The whole land lacked shadows or relief, but for the corn and a bloom of light on the tops of the beech trees in the wood above Long Croft.

They worked the afternoon.

"Whet!" shouted Ozzie.

Kivvers and stubble followed the men, round and round, the square spiral tightened on the field.

At baggin time Uncle Charlie came down to see how Robert had managed. He looked at the grass and earth.

"I said smooth it, youth, not build a flipping parapet."

"Well, cob you!" shouted Robert. "Cob you, then!"

And he stuck his spade in the ground and ran down the field to Faddock Allman. Uncle Charlie followed with the beer. He was smiling. Robert lay under the hedge, batting at flies with his hands.

Faddock Allman and Uncle Charlie drank, and Uncle Charlie passed the stone jar to Robert. "There's more to feckazing than feckazing, isn't there, youth?" he said.

"It's these clegs," said Robert. "They're eating me."

"Clegs don't bite," said Uncle Charlie. "They've got hot feet."

The sweat dried.

"But, without you've a trade, feckazing is all you'll get," said Uncle Charlie.

"I want more stone," said Faddock Allman.

"Then you can want," said Uncle Charlie, and polished the stock of his rifle.

"Where are you working?" said Robert.

"Oh, all over," said Uncle Charlie. "Wherever there's call. Plug Street, mostly."

"Where's that?" said Robert.

"Aback of Leah's Hill," said Uncle Charlie.

"How do you get there?" said Robert.

"Train. Then boat. It costs nowt. The King pays. Then another train. Then you walk it. Past Dicky Bush and Roody Boys, over Hazy Brook, till you come to Funky Villas. Turn left for Moo-Cow Farm, and Plug Street's second on the right."

"You're twitting me," said Robert.

"But that's where I'll be working, Tuesday," said Uncle Charlie. "Plug Street."

"Is it a journey?" said Robert.

"It is when you're carrying full pack," said Uncle Charlie. "But I reckon I'll go a shorter way, meself. I reckon I just about shall. I might just go the aimer gate this time. I've done enough traipsing."

"All in!" shouted Ozzie Leah.

Uncle Charlie and Robert went back up the field. It was still hot, but the sun was redder.

Robert took all the turf off the jackacre and curved its line and shallowed it. Then he put the turf back. He watched the reapers. They moved more gentle than the chapel clock.

"Whet!" shouted Ozzie.

There was a square of corn uncut in the middle of the field. Ozzie and Young Ollie sharpened up, but Uncle Charlie came down to the corner by the gate where Robert was, and laid his scythe against the hedge.

Robert pointed to the jackacre. "Will it do?" he said.

"Ay. It'll do," said Uncle Charlie. "Now fetch Faddock Allman and me rifle."

Robert went down the hill on Wicked Winnie, using his heels.

"Mister Allman," he said, "me Uncle Charlie wants you, and we're to take him his rifle."

Faddock Allman swung himself into Wicked Winnie and picked up the rifle wrapped in sacking. "All present and correct!" he shouted. "Mount!"

Robert put the sashcord across his shoulders and climbed the field. His boots were still slippery, and Faddock Allman was so heavy that Robert had to zig-zag along the hill. "You can go where you please, you can shin up trees," sang Faddock Allman at every turn, "but you can't get away from the guns!" Robert was sobbing with sweat by the time he reached the top field.

"Number Six-six Battery, Royal Field Artillery, ready for inspection! Sir!" shouted Faddock Allman.

Uncle Charlie didn't answer. He was on his heel, chewing a straw of stubble, and looking at the standing corn. His face had gone different. It was thinner, and Robert couldn't tell what was in the eyes. He spat the straw out and drank from a flask he carried in his pocket, enough to wet his mouth, no more.

Uncle Charlie stood up. He took the rifle. "Get aback of me," he said.

Robert made Wicked Winnie safe with chocks of stone. Faddock Allman pushed his helmet off his forehead. The men and boys were standing around the square of corn, and were silent. The women had moved away down the hill.

"Ready?" Ozzie Leah called.

Uncle Charlie nodded. He loaded the magazine with real bullets, grey iron and brass, clipped the magazine into the rifle, put another bullet in the breech and rattled the bolt. He held the rifle across his body; pointing to the earth, flexed his shoulders and breathed deeply, and then was still.

Ozzie Leah looked at Uncle Charlie once more, raised his hand, his cap in it, and brought it down.

"Who-whoop! Wo-whoop! Wo-o-o-o! Who-whoop! Wo-whoop! Wo-o-o-o!" The men and boys yelled the cry. They yelled and yelled and clapped their hands and waved their caps and banged sticks together. Uncle Charlie didn't move. "Who-whoop! Wo-whoop! Wo-o-o-o!" The noise was tremendous.

But through the noise came another, a scream, a squeal, and, in terror, rabbits broke out of the last standing corn. All day they had worked inward from the scythes, and now they ran. Uncle Charlie watched. Over the field, between the kivvers, dodging, driven by noise, the rabbits went and their screaming pierced all noise.

Uncle Charlie swung the rifle to his shoulder, turning on his hips. He fired. The sound of the rifle deadened Robert's ears. Left. Left. Right. Left. "Who-whoop! Wo-whoop! Wo-o-o-o!" Right.

One rabbit was going uphill, in line with the men. Uncle Charlie watched it go until it climbed above them. The rabbit was at the top cornerpost of the field when he shot it.

The others got away. Their squealing stopped when they reached the bracken of the wood.

And Saint Philip's church was still black, and there were no shadows.

Ozzie Leah shouted, "Good lad, Sniper!"

Robert looked at Uncle Charlie. The face was no different. "When there's too many," said Uncle Charlie, "you can't tell them from poppies. They're all alike the same, you see."

"Cop hold, Sniper," said Ozzie Leah. "Three for you, and a sixpence for the bullets." He had brought the rabbits down to Uncle Charlie. They had all been shot in the head, and none of the meat was spoilt, though the heads had gone. "Me and Ollie can finish," said Ozzie Leah. "You get off home, there's a good lad."

"Ay," said Uncle Charlie.

He took the three rabbits and the spade and the sashcord and his rifle and walked off the hill, as if Faddock Allman was leading him, like a big dog. And Robert followed.

They sat by the heap of road flint stone and gutted the rabbits. Uncle Charlie lifted his eyes to look at the work he had done, at the harvest got.

"That's my trade, Dick-Richard," said Uncle Charlie. "I stop rabbits skriking. There's me craft, and there's my masterness."

They wiped their hands on grass. Together Robert and Uncle Charlie pulled Faddock Allman as far as the house. At the gate, Robert carried the hammers in to the end room while Uncle Charlie went to fetch Faddock Allman his brew for the night. Father was finishing supper. Mother began to skin the rabbits.

Uncle Charlie boiled out his rifle, dried it and cleaned it and took it into the kitchen. He sat down at the table.

"Now then, Joseph," said Uncle Charlie.

"Now then, Charlie," said Father.

They looked at each other, and they laughed.

The corn kivvers waited on three church bells. The last cry went up, "Who-whoop! Wo-whoop! Wo-o-o-o!" and was quiet at

Leah's Hill. Wicked Winnie took Faddock Allman home. Father and Uncle Charlie played the great tune of the Hough, E Flat cornet and rifle, on either side of the fire, and the day swung in the chapel clock, escapement to the sun.

TOM FOBBLE'S DAY

TOM FOBBLE'S DAY

"Tom Fobble's Day!"

The first snowball caught William in the teeth. The second burst on his forehead; the third on his balaclava helmet.

He let go of his sledge, and ran, blindly. The snowballs kept hitting him, on the back, on the legs, softly, quietly, but he couldn't stand them.

The snow gathered between the iron of his clogs and the curved wood of the sole and built into rockers of ice. His ankles twisted and he fell over, trying not to cry. He curled himself against the attack.

But it had stopped. He opened his eyes. He wasn't even out of range. Stewart Allman had stopped throwing and was sitting on William's sledge.

William stood up. "Give us me sledge!" It had taken him a day and a morning to build it out of an old crate.

"It isn't yours," said Stewart Allman.

"It is!"

"It isn't. I've Tom Fobbled it."

"You can't! You can't Tom Fobble sledges! Only marbles!"

"What are you going to do about it?" said Stewart Allman.

"And only after Easter!" William was getting more angry than he was scared.

"It is after Easter," said Stewart Allman. "Last Easter!" He laughed.

William charged. The snow on his clogs made him trip, and he rolled down the hill and Stewart Allman sat on him.

"Easter! Tom Fobble's Day's Easter and marbles! You know it is!"

Stewart Allman pushed a handful of snow into William's mouth.

"I only want to lend it, you boiled ha'penny," he said. "We'll take it in turns."

"Where's yours?" said William.

"Bust," said Stewart Allman.

Lizzie Leah's was the place where everybody went to sledge. It was two fields, one above the other and above the road. The bottom field was short and steep, and all that had to be done was to stop before the thorn hedge. The top field was long, and there was a gate in the corner to the bottom field. But there weren't many who could sledge the top field, corner to corner, across the slope, and through the gate and down the bottom field.

It was fast, and the sledge had to be turned sharply for the gate, and at the only patch in the whole field where it could be turned, there was a hump that made the sledge take off. And the chances for the sledge then were to land against a tree, or in barbed wire, or the gatepost, or to go through to the bottom field.

"I'll swap you," said William.

"What for?" said Stewart Allman.

"An incendiary," said William.

"Show us."

William pulled the incendiary bomb out of his jacket inside pocket. He had found it that morning, after the air raid. The bomb was the shape of a bicycle pump, but corroded and sticky, like an old battery.

"OK," said Stewart Allman. "I'll swap."

He pulled both his trouser pockets out, and two piles of shrapnel dropped into the snow. "Hot last night," he said. Shrapnel picked up hot from the gunfire was worth more than cold-found. "Give us the sledge."

"I meant swap you instead of lending," said William.

"I didn't," said Stewart Allman.

"You'll bust it," said William.

"You have first go, then," said Stewart Allman.

William collected up the shrapnel. It was a jagged, brown metal, sharp enough to cut and to pierce, and even its surface was harsh, like sand.

"All right," he said. He put the shrapnel in his jacket, and walked along the bottom field to where the girls had a sledge run.

"Top field," said Stewart Allman.

Stewart Allman's sledge had disintegrated against the tree. William went a few yards above the hump and turned his sledge round.

"Is that all you're doing?" said Stewart Allman.

"It's new," said William. He lay down on the sledge. It was no longer than his chest, and his head stuck out.

"Want a shove?" said Stewart Allman.

William got up and sat on the sledge, holding the string.

"You're frit," said Stewart Allman.

"Don't care," said William. He pushed with his feet. The sledge moved and sank into the snow and stopped. He tried again, and slipped forward off the front of the sledge. The third time, the thin, flat runners passed over the ridge of snow they had built, and William was away.

He wasn't going fast enough at the hump, and had to heel himself along to get over. He rode down the bottom field and braked before he reached the hedge.

"How is it?" Stewart Allman shouted.

"Smashing!"

William pulled the sledge back up the hill. Stewart Allman had climbed to the middle of the top field and was waiting. The middle of the top field was as high as it was safe for the best sledgers to go. William had to stop to knock the snow off his clogs.

"Don't be all day," said Stewart Allman.

"You've got boots," said William.

"What's that cissy way of riding?" said Stewart Allman.

"It's my sledge," said William.

"You look a right betty."

Stewart Allman lay on the sledge and bent his knees. "Shove us," he said.

William took hold of Stewart Allman's feet and ran as if he was pushing a cart.

"Let go!"

William fell over.

The rickety crate bobbed down the field. William thought it would shake to pieces, but it didn't. He saw it hit the hump and turn in the air. Stewart Allman had his foot down hard just before he left the ground. He was through the gate and out of sight behind the hedge between the fields.

William waited. He heard a cry.

"You what?" he shouted.

He heard the cry again, but couldn't tell what Stewart Allman was saying.

He set off down the field, following the tracks. They turned at the hump and there was a gap before they began again. The brow of the bottom field hid the road hedge. If there had been an accident there was no one else on Lizzie Leah's to help him.

But Stewart Allman was sitting by the hedge. He had pulled up exactly right. The marks of his toecaps had dug down to the frozen grass to brake him. The lines of green looked wrong in the snow.

"What's up?" said William.

"Nowt," said Stewart Allman. "It's your turn."

"Why couldn't you bring it back?" said William.

"It's not mine," said Stewart Allman.

"You should've fetched it!"

Stewart Allman began to make snow-balls.

William took his turn from the same place as before, but kicked harder and had enough speed to ride the hump. At the bottom he waited for Stewart Allman, but he didn't come, so William went back up the field.

"One more," said William, "then I'm off."

"What doing?"

"I must go see me Grandad."

"Why now?"

"I must catch him while he's at work. And anyroad, it's going to snow a blizzard."

"You can't tell that," said Stewart Allman. "Sun's shining."

"It isn't at the back of Saint Philip's," said William.

The sky was clear, but behind the church and across the plain there was a cloud that made the seagulls white against it, and the weathercock on the church was golden.

"Snow's not that colour," said Stewart Allman. "Snow's not black. You're daft."

"It's still last goes," said William.

"I tell you what," said Stewart Allman. "You lie on top of me, and I'll steer, and we'll get a fair old baz up with that weight."

"No," said William.

"Are you frit again?"

"It'd squash your gas mask."

"Mardy!" said Stewart Allman, and ran down the hill, pushing the sledge in front of him. When he could run no faster he dived on and was away.

As he reached top speed, just before the hump, the left hand runner began to squirm. Even William could see the movement. Stewart Allman tried to brake, but couldn't, and he lost direction by putting both toes down. The runner cracked, and the sledge lifted into the air sideways, and Stewart Allman rolled with it so that the sledge was between him and the gatepost. William heard the crunch and the smash and was already running. The shrapnel chimed in his pockets.

"I've bent me incendiary," said Stewart Allman. "Whatever made you think that was a sledge?" He held the splintered boxwood dangling together on lengths of tin. "Two wrecked in one day's not bad, is it? Shall you be coming after tea?"

"How can I, now you've bust me sledge?" said William.

"Oh, there'll be plenty tonight," said Stewart Allman, "never fret. And it's a bomber's moon: should be good."

"I'll have to see," said William.

"Play again, then?" said Stewart Allman.

"Play again," said William.

William left his sledge on the pile of other broken sledges and set off for the village.

Grandad's house was at the bottom of Lizzie Leah's, and it was a measured mile from the house to where he worked. William tried to pace it, one thousand seven hundred and sixty strides, but his stride wasn't a yard long and the snow packed under his clogs, and the wind came with the blizzard out of the cloud.

The worst part of sledging was always after. The flakes melted in his balaclava, and he had to keep sucking the chinpiece to keep it from rubbing sore. His mouth tasted of sweet wool. He drew his hands up inside his jacket sleeves, but his khaki mittens were wet. His trousers chafed below his knees, and his sock garters were tight. Each kneecap was blue.

The air raid siren sounded the alert. The alert often went during the day, although the bombers came only at night.

William crossed the village street in frog-hops and giant-strides to reach the grid above the ironmonger's cellar where Grandad worked. He made it: one thousand seven hundred and sixty yards, jumps and strides.

William stood on the grid. He could see Grandad's bench below, and the silver gleam of his hair.

William sniffed the drop off his nose. He was cold. He dragged his feet sideways across the grating, to free his clogs, but all he did was to push loose snow onto Grandad's window.

"Oh, flipping heck," said William.

He had been watching the silver of Grandad's hair: now he was looking at his blue eyes and sharp red nose.

He went into the empty shop. The bell tinkled on its curled spring.

At the back of the shop there was a yard door that slid in grooves. William could open it with one finger, because Grandad had made a lead counterweight and hung it by a sashcord, so that the door was balanced. Behind the big green door was the farrier's yard, where horses used to be shod, and from the yard broad steps went down to Grandad's cellar and forge and the flat, square cobbles.

It was for ever dark at the forge. Light came from the grating and made silhouettes of all the heavy gear; the hoists, the tackle, the presses, the anvils and the skirt of the forge hood.

Coals burned dull red. Under the grating was the bench where Grandad sat. He was the whitesmith and locksmith, and black-smith, too.

His crucible stood in a firebrick bed, full of solder. His irons were by him, some so big that lifting them made William's wrists ache. But he had seen Grandad take them, and heat them, and when they were hot, Grandad spat on them; and the spit danced, and he ran his thumb along the end to test the heat.

And then he took metal and did wonder-ful things; turning, twisting, tapping, shaping, dabbing and making; quickly, before the metals were cold. Brew-cans, billy-cans, milk-cans, and the great churns that stood at the roadside. He could make them all. And he could make brass fenders straight, and take the dents from tin, and put back the fragile lion-masks on coal scuttles.

"I've a month's mind to tan your hide," said Grandad. "What were you standing out there for, fair starved, and the siren blahting?"

"It's a false alarm," said William. "Or snow got into it."

"And what if somebody doesn't tell Gerry one of these days, and he finds you gawping up at him?" said Grandad.

"That's what I've come for," said William. "We have to have our names written in indelible on all our clothes, and Mum says can you stamp mine on me clogs, please?"

Grandad put his tools down and looked at William. William swung his gas mask tin off his shoulder and sat on it.

"And what's the indelible in aid of?" said Grandad.

"We were told in prayers. We've to be ready for inspection on Monday, or else."

"I see," said Grandad. "And what are you doing clagged up so you can't hardly walk?"

"I keep stopping to scrawk it off," said William.

"Come here," said Grandad. "I don't know. What do they learn you these days?"

William leant against the bench and Grandad put a clog between his knees, with his back to William, as if he was shoeing a horse, and knocked the snow off with a hammer.

"Hold still," he said, and he reached over to where his metal punches stood in their rack in order of the alphabet, and very deftly he took each as he needed it, placed the letter against the sole of William's clog and tapped it. The punch left a clean print in the wood. And he dropped the punch back in the rack, and took another.

Grandad finished William's name on one clog, and swapped legs.

"I reckon," said Grandad, "that in fifty-five years of setting labels on milk-cans for farmers, I must've come near writing a book with these. And now I'm stamping you up so as we can go looking for what's left of you next time you gawp at bombers.

I don't know. I really do not know. Hold still, will you?"

He dipped a worn paint brush into a tin and daubed something stiff and smooth over the soles of William's clogs. "There," he said, "that'll keep the snow off. But mind how you treat your Mother's rugs, or she'll play the dickens with the both of us."

"What is it?" said William.

"Axle grease."

William sat down by the forge again. "Can you do anything for the leathers?" he said. "They're that stiff all the time, I have to warm them to take them off. They're crippling me."

"Worse could happen," said Grandad. "Bad shoes have saved my life."

"How?" said William.

"In Kaiser Bill's War," said Grandad. "I went for me medical, along with all the other youths from this shop; Tommy Latham, David Peters and them. But the army doctor said as how he reckoned they could manage without me. He said, 'You've hammer toes.' And I said, 'What do you expect? I'm a smith!' But it was a terrible rough auction, was Kaiser Bill's War. Men were going thick and threefold. Like water down a ditch.

"They're all on the Memorial at Saint Philip's. George Powell, Oliver Leah, the Burgesses; Fred, Jim, Percy, Reg. And me own half-brother, Charlie. He's there. And he was the one me Mother reared. For that."

The forge was low, but warm enough to chill William's clothes with melting.

The all-clear sounded. William and Grandad looked through the window, criss-crossed with strips of brown paper against blast. The blizzard had stopped.

"I brought these down from up home this morning," said Grandad.

He went to a row of vices clamped to a bench. In the vices were two strips of iron, about six feet long, and bevelled on one side. Grandad had drilled holes in each strip and countersunk them.

"Get on the bellows, youth," he said.

William began to work the lever handle of the forge bellows up and down. It was as though the cellar was waking, breathing. The coals glowed more brightly, and blue gasses licked around them.

Up and down, up and down. The warmth came back.

"Steady," said Grandad. "We're not the Queen Elizabeth, nor Chapel organ, neither. Steady. Keep her going gentle."

He held an end of one of the strips in the forge. When the end was cherry red he lifted it over to his swage block.

In all Grandad's forge and cellar there was nothing like the swage block. It was a square, thick slab, too heavy for William even to move, but Grandad could move it. Its edges were indented, but each indentation was a different size, a different shape.

They were slots, for bevels or angles. And the block itself was pierced by squares and circles, so that the weight looked light, and in one corner was a hollow, a circular dish when the block lay that way.

It was a shape older than anvils.

Yet it was only a block of iron, to be used any side up, for anything that was useful.

Grandad put the hot end into a hole in the swage block, and pulled down until the strip began to bend. He drew it out a short way, and bent it again. The metal was losing its colour.

"Now," said Grandad. "Give her a good un! Come on! Queen Elizabeth, Chapel and all!"

The lever went up and down, and William with it. The forge roared. Grandad held the strip with long pincers and paddled it in the fire. He kept looking at the bellows handle, as if he was measuring it, but most of the time he was watching the heated iron.

"You'll often wonder why a smith works in the dark," he said, "and here's why. It's nothing dubious. You can't judge colour if the sun's putting your fire out. It's pale straw we're after; pale straw, and not a touch lighter. See!"

He pulled out the strip. Where he had bent it in the swage block was yellow but not white. He moved quickly now and turned the rough bend in the hollow cup, pressing but not forcing the softened iron to the perfect curve, so that the cup in the block gave its shape to his hand. Then he laid the strip aside. It changed from straw to cherry.

"We'll not need to quench it," he said.

Grandad took the second strip and did the same to that as he had done to the first, until the two were side by side, identical.

"Leave her now," he said to William. "She'll do."

The fire receded. Grandad flicked the

swage block clean with the end of his leather brat, and wiped his face. He sat with William by the forge and drew two cups of beer from the barrel he kept under his bench.

William drank, and watched.

"I'll tell you something," said Grandad. "When I was a young youth, and wed, we had the Boer War. And I was playing E Flat cornet for the Temperance Band. And every time we killed two Boers we had us a carnival. Well, there came this night when we'd killed three, and didn't we celebrate! Charlie and me, we were that fresh we had to play leaning against the wall. And Ollie Leah was sat on the floor there, out in the middle of the road. He played the big drum, and they said as he was the only one to keep time sat down. I suppose there's a Memorial to them Boers somewhere, if we only knew. But there was no wireless, you see.

"Now in Kaiser Bill's War we were working all hours on horse shoes. And that was on top of the regular jobs. I shifted fifteen ton of shoe iron myself. And fifteen ton is thirty-three thousand six hundred shoes. Eight thousand four hundred horses. It took us all our time."

Grandad threw the last drops of beer into the fire, and wiped his moustache. He bounced the two strips against the palm of his hand. They were cool. He pulled the bellows handle down and laid each strip along the wood. The iron was a perfect fit, lying close, and curving with the end.

Grandad pushed the handle up once and pulled it down again. The bellows breathed and the fire brightened. Grandad stood up and unbolted the handle. He took the long wood to the bench, laid it carefully, and bent to examine the grain. Then he took a chisel and held it to the wood, and he hit the chisel with a hammer. There was a sound like muslin tearing, and the handle ripped, split apart down its length, clean as if a saw had done it.

"That's a good bit of ash," said Grandad. "I thought it was, the first day I set eyes on it."

"But what are you doing?" said William.

"Doing? I've done."

Grandad and William stood in the cellar. Light was going from window and fire.

"Fifty-five years," said Grandad. "I reckon it's best left now. Did you not know it was me last day?"

William shook his head.

"Come on," said Grandad. "We've a job to finish."

He went to his bench. His irons and punches were ready for work. Everywhere was clean in the dirt. He untied his brat from round his waist, used it to flick the anvils, the vices, the bench and the swage block of dust, and hung it on a nail. His hand touched everything once.

"She'll do," said Grandad.

Grandad and William went out of the cellar up the steps to the farrier's yard. Grandad's bicycle was in the yard. He tied the iron and the split handle onto the frame, put on his cap and his trouser clips, wheeled the bicycle into the street, and locked the door.

"There," he said. He gave William the key. It was so worn that the teeth were smooth, the whole key thin from wearing out pockets.

"It was me first prentice piece. I cut a new one just before the sirens went. That's a lifetime for you."

William held the key. It was metal like a pebble from the brook. Every part was soft and rounded, without edges. He wrapped it in his handkerchief, so that the shrapnel wouldn't scratch it.

Grandad switched on his front and rear lamps, and mounted the bicycle.

"Jump up," he said, "and we'll go home

and make ourselves some tea."

William sat on the carrier over the back mudguard. He had one arm around Grandad and the other over the bellows handle.

Grandad pushed off and began his ride home. He always went at the same pace, steadily, ignoring hills.

"Hold still," he said, "else you'll have us in the ditch."

But it was hard. The carrier was sharp, the wind cold, and there was nowhere for William's feet. He had to let them hang wide of the wheel. The tyres swished on the packed snow. His face was in Grandad's coat, and he could feel the movement of pedalling through the heavy folds. The leather saddle squeaked and its springs copied the road.

"Near enough," said Grandad, "with it being a measured mile, and allowing four trips a day until I lost your Grandma, and two a day since, what with not coming home for dinner, I calculate I've biked this road for work equivalent to two and a half times round the world at the equator."

It was night when they reached home, but the snow reflected the rising moon on the thatch and the whitewashed walls.

Grandad put his bicycle in the coalshed and shovelled a bucket of coal to last the evening. They went into the house and hung the blackout curtains over the windows before they lit the lamps. Grandad poked the fire. He had banked it up with slack before going to work, and the coaldust was glowing under the dead surface.

"I'll put the kettle on and wash me," said Grandad, "while you go and fetch some spuds in."

William took a basket from the kitchen and went to the garden.

The potatoes had been hogged for the winter. The hogg was a shallow pit, big as a room, and the potatoes were stacked in it, pitched like a roof to throw the rain off, covered with soil and bracken to keep out the cold.

William pulled the bracken away from the hogg where it had been opened, filled the basket, and covered the hogg again.

When he was back inside the house he took off his balaclava and mittens and put them on the fender to dry.

Grandad was washing his hands in a tin basin. William turned on the tap over the slopstone. "Get the muck off and leave the jackets," said Grandad. "We'll have them in the oven."

William tugged the earth away in frozen lumps. "There's a yard of frost out there," he said. "Grandad?"

"Ay?"

"What if somebody shouts Tom Fobble's Day on you and it's not for marbles and you're not after Easter?"

"Is he bigger than you?" said Grandad.

"Yes."

"Then run like beggary."

"It's Stewart Allman," said William. "He took me sledge and wrecked it."

"And good riddance," said Grandad. "I never saw such a codge."

Grandad wiped his hands on the harsh towel. William held the potatoes under the tap. A ball of earth came away solid. He broke it open in his hands.

"Eh up!" said Grandad.

The earth was like a split rock. In the middle of the black ball, clean, white, shining, was a clay pipe. The pipe was decorated in fluted lines, and was un-damaged.

William laid the earth gently on the slopstone and let the water trickle from the tap. He took a piece of shrapnel out of his pocket and used its jagged point to help the earth loose.

"Let's have a look," said Grandad.

"Wait. Don't touch," said William. Grandad's hands had reached to feel the pipe, but they were now too big; they were too clumsy for the job.

Grandad leaned on the slopstone and watched William.

"That's a Macclesfield dandy. I've seen me Grandfather smoke one many a time. But I've never seen one not broken sooner or later. It must be his: and in the garden all this while, and not hurt."

The last of the soil was out of the bowl and William unblocked the stem. He blew it clear. And then he sucked, breathed in. The air rasped through the stem.

William washed his hands. The soap was yellow, bone-shaped, sharp with earth. The grit stood out.

Grandad put four potatoes in the oven. "We'll get ourselves fettled while they're baking," he said.

He picked up a torch and went outside. At the end of the house there was a low room built on. Grandad kept rubbish in it. The house was old, and nothing was ever thrown away, because, with so much rubbish over so many years, some of it was always useful.

A jumble of iron and wood lay in a corner. It was the remains of a loom. William could remember when it stood upright and he used to play on it. But all the softwood was worm-eaten, and one day it had collapsed under him.

The iron was newly bright from a saw. It was the iron that Grandad had curved in the swage block to the bellows handle.

"Catch hold on these," Grandad pulled some rags out of a drawer and gave them to William. They were soft and slippery. When he squeezed them they crumpled up small, but sprang open as soon as he let go.

Grandad dismantled what was left of the loom, choosing only the good oak. The rest he smashed to kindling with his boot. "I've been meaning to rimson this glory-hole for years," he said. "It's got you can't move, there's that much clutter."

Grandad and William carried the oak into the house. Grandad brewed the tea, and searched out an empty tobacco tin.

"Put Grandfather's pipe in that," he said, "and pack it round with them rags against it getting broken."

"What must I do with it?" said William.

"Keep it," said Grandad' "You found it: I didn't. But let it lay there, so as I can see at it a while.".

He opened the oven door and pulled out the potatoes, and he sat with William, and they ate them with salt and drank the tea. The potatoes were burnt black on one side and raw the other. Grandad kept looking at the pipe and shaking his head. He was laughing.

"And it was in the tater hogg?" he said.

"Must've been," said William.

"It figures," said Grandad.

"How?" said William.

"He was a rum un," said Grandad. "What you might call a Sunday Saint and a Monday Devil. It was his music, you see. Oh, he was the only best ringer and singer for miles, and he played every instrument he could lay hand to. Sunday at Chapel, regular. But Monday, and he was down your throat before you could open your mouth. Nothing vindictive, though. And I never did hear him swear. Not that he couldn't. What! He knew the words, right enough. He could've sworn tremendous. He could've sworn the cross off an ass's back. But he never did. He never had to. His mind was that quick. And he did love to argue. Choose what you said, he'd put the other side, even when he agreed with you. And another thing: there wasn't one could take his drink as well as that old youth: there wasn't!"

Grandad pushed the dishes aside and opened his toolbox. William covered the pipe, closed the lid and put the tin in his pocket, by the key. Grandad set the two lengths of split ash handle on the table and laid the bent iron next to them. He stuck the poker in the fire and wedged it between the bars of the grate. Then he sorted through the loom wood, made a stack of pieces, and marked them off all the same length with a foot rule and a pencil.

When all was tidy he began to work.

He used the table as a bench, and cut the marked oak on the line with a tenon saw. He started each cut by drawing the saw backwards, towards him, three times. Then he was away, cutting true, his hand and thumb clamped to the wood and the table.

"He used to go busking for beer, round and about!" Grandad laughed again. "Him and old Bob Sumner, Joe Swindells and Tom Wood. They were the Hough Band, of a Sunday, playing hymns. But the rest of the week they called theirselves the Hough Fizzers. And didn't they pop!"

He had cut the oak into eighteen inch lengths. He fixed the two halves of ash that distance apart, and parallel, and nailed a length of oak across at the bottom of the curve of the handle. Behind it he put another; and so he went on. He worked without waste, and easily. The nails went into the oak and ash without bending.

"Well, one night, they'd had a right good night round the farms, and they were on their way back from The Bull's Head at Mottram, very fresh, and they come to a quickthorn hedge, and the other side of it was a potato hogg as belonged to Jesse Leah.

"Now old Jesse, he'd stuck a twothree pieces of stove pipe through the top, with a little cowl on it, to ventilate the middle of the hogg, you see.

"Well, just then, up comes the moon behind the hogg and the bit of stove pipe, and Grandfather, he says, 'Wait on,' he says. 'Some there are going to bed. Let's give them a tune!' And they serenaded that potato hogg till morning. But Grandmother! Didn't she give him some stick, at after!"

Grandad turned the whole frame over, picked up the two strips of iron and fitted them. He took a screw, held it in one of the countersunk holes and drove it home. Now, for the first time, Grandad could be seen to be working. He grunted and sweated, and didn't talk. His grip on the screwdriver made his spark-pocked hand white, and once a screw started to bite he kept it turning without rest until its head was flush with the iron.

But when he stood back, there was a sledge.

He sawed off the ends of the bellows handle that was now two runners level with the end of the iron that shod them.

Grandad left the sledge and came to sit in his chair by the fire. He rubbed his forehead.

"You mustn't let them screws stop turning," he said, "else they'll stick for evermore, and you'll not shift them. They'll shear, first."

He examined the poker. "Keep him that colour," he said. He opened the corner cupboard above his chair. It was full of string and rope. He chose a length of rope, sashcord, like the sashcord that held the counterweight of the yard door above the cellar.

Grandad spat on the poker, tested its whiteness with his thumb, pressed it against the upcurve of one of the runners. The wood hissed and smoked, and the poker sank through. When it cooled, Grandad reheated it and pressed again. The room was full of the sweet smell of ash. There was a hole in the curve, like a black-rimmed eye.

Grandad burnt through the other runner, threaded the cord into both eyes, knotted the ends, and the sledge was complete.

"Is that for me?" said William, not daring to.

"Well, it's not for me!" said Grandad.

"For me own? For me very liggy own?"

"Ay. Get that up Lizzie Leah's and see what Allmans have to say. Loom and forge."

Grandad threw the scrap wood on the coals. It sent flames of every colour into the chimney. "They'll take no harm," said Grandad. "It's sparks you must watch. Once they set in the thatch the whole roof can fly on fire."

William leaned over the hearth to look up the chimney. The sparks spiralled and died in the blackness. But there was something bright, reflecting flame.

"Grandad?"

"Ay?"

"There's two horse shoes hanging in the chimney."

"I know there is," said Grandad.

"But they're clean. There's no soot on them."

"I know there isn't."

William reached into the chimney with his hand.

"Leave them," said Grandad. "They're not for you. Not yet."

"What are they?"

"Me and your Grandma's wedding."

"Up the chimney?" said William.

"Of course they're up the chimney," said Grandad. "Of course they're clean. I put them there forty-two years ago, and I clean them of a Sunday. What are you staring like a throttled earwig for?"

"I didn't know," said William.

"You didn't know?" said Grandad. "A high-learnt youth like you didn't know? Your Grandma and me, we'd have let every stick of furniture go first, and the house, before we'd have parted from them. They're our wedding. They're your Father and your Uncles. They're you. Do you not see? They're us!

"Your friends and your neighbours give them to the wedding. No one says. It happens. And it happens as the smith's at his forge one night, and happens to find the money by the door. And he makes the shoes alone, swage block and anvil: and we put them in the chimney piece. Mind you, I'd know Tommy Latham's work anywhere. But we don't let on. It's all a mystery. Now get up them fields."

There were voices in the road. William put on his balaclava and mittens.

Grandad lifted the sledge down. "She'll stick a toucher at first," he said, "while the iron finds a polish. But then she'll go, with that bevel to her. And at after, all she'll want is a spot of oil, against rust in summer.

"I feel the wind's bristled up," he said. "I'll not come out."

William went down the path from the house: Grandad closed the blackout behind him.

The sledge jerked a little at first, and left stains that showed in the moonlight, but the curved, strong iron, countersunk screwed, rode on the frost better than the tin runners of the broken crate had done. The swage block down in the cellar worked on the hill.

Lizzie Leah's was crowded. People were coming from both directions along the road. William pulled the sledge up the bottom field. It was heavy, but the rope didn't cut, and it was all strong and in balance and carried a lot of its own weight.

There were more of the bigger boys at night, and they racketed over the hump. William had to dodge through the gateway between runs. There was the flurried rattle of approach, the gasp in the air and the beat of the landing. William set himself above the hump; but before he could start, a sledge came at him from above, veered to the barbed wire, and the rider skidded off, over the hump and through the gate.

It was Stewart Allman.

They were coming in twos and threes and even in packs; starting together and racing for the gate.

Stewart Allman whistled through his fingers. "Wait on!" he shouted up the hill. "We've a betty!"

William sat on the sledge, looked over his shoulder, but there was no one coming, so he heeled himself forward.

The sledge moved gently, surely, sensitive to touch. He could steer it, and just as he had felt the road and the bicycle through the slow movement of Grandad's coat, he felt the hill through the sledge, as if he flowed over it, never left it. There were no jolts. The sledge crushed ruts and ran only on the true hill.

"Where've you got that from?" said Stewart Allman.

"Me Grandad," said William. "He made it."

"Let's have a go," said Stewart Allman.

They were walking back. The axle grease on William's clogs let no snow gather. Now Stewart Allman was trying to keep up

"Barley mey fog shot no back bargains," said William.

"I only want a go; just one."

"You pull it, then," said William, and gave the rope to Stewart Allman.

"Eh! What's it made of?"

"Oak, mostly," said William.

"It weighs a ton," said Stewart Allman.

He was out of breath when they reached the middle of the top field.

He lay on the sledge, with the rope tucked under him, and gripped the runners where they curled up at the end of the forge bellows handle. The sledge was longer than he was.

"Give us a shove."

But the sledge began to move as soon as Stewart Allman lifted his feet. It didn't snatch or creak or waver. It moved straight down and across the hill, and so marvellously that it was only when the other sledgers, climbing back, stopped to watch it pass them that William realised how fast it was going.

Stewart Allman made no noise. The sledge hit the hump and reared and stood on end. William heard the runners twang the barbed wire, and the sledge and Stewart Allman disappeared.

William jumped down the field sideways, using his clog irons to grip. He found the sledge. It had snapped the wire. Stewart Allman was in a snow drift.

William grabbed the sledge. "You're not safe!" he yelled. "You might've bust this one, too, you daft beggar!"

He ran up the hill, pulling the undamaged sledge. He staggered and ran, angry, unthinking. But he had to stop when he came to the corner post of the top of the field: the top of the top field, where nobody went.

William turned the sledge against the hill, and sat down.

He watched the others. They couldn't see him by the stump. He watched moon and starlight and shapes gliding. Another cloud was coming from the north, but it was a long way off.

The air raid sirens sounded the alert, village after village, spreading like bonfires. He settled down to watch.

As soon as the bombers were heard, the searchlights would be switched on and the guns would start to fire. They were in Johnny Baguley's field, less than a mile away.

"Eh! You! Public Enemy Number One! We're waiting!"

It was Stewart Allman.

William looked down. The next highest sledge was a long way below him. He could crawl under the fence and down the other side of the hill, but Stewart Allman would know. William would be ambushed.

The field was waiting. Dark patches looking at him.

He stood up and tugged the sledge round. As soon as it was in line with the slope it began to move. He shortened the rope.

William sat astride, his heels braced. He let out the rope, lay back, and eased the pressure off his heels. He felt the sledge start, and then he felt no speed, only a rhythm of the hill. The sledge found its own course; a touch corrected it. As he went faster, William used his clogs for balance. The steering moved into his hands and arms, then his shoulders, and then he was going so fast and so true that he could steer with a turn of his head.

The watching groups were a flicker as he passed, and his speed grew on the more trampled snow.

He saw the hump and the gate, but saw nothing to fear. He took in more rope, gripped, and the forge bellows runners breasted the air without shock. He pulled on the rope and kiltered his head to the right. His weight had brought him forward and the curved runners were at his shoulder.

Then the trailing corners of the loom iron took the weight, the front of the sledge dropped away, and William was lying back again, coasting along the bottom field.

He put down his heels and stopped at the hedge.

Stewart Allman arrived.

"Any bones broken?" he said.

"No," said William.

"We thought you'd be killed."

"Get off with you!" said William. "It's dead safe. Me Grandad made it."

"Will you go again?" said Stewart Allman. "From the top."

"It's a heck of a climb," said William.

"I'll give you a pull to half way," said Stewart Allman.

"What about your sledge?"

"It's no weight. Honest. Will you?"

"OK."

Stewart Allman took both sledges and floundered up the field. William dusted off the snow powder that had sprayed over him in a plume.

"He's going again!" said Stewart Allman when they reached the others. "Stand
back!"

He handed over the rope to William, and
William went on alone.

"I was going to, anyway," he said when
he was at the top.

He set off. It had not been imagined.
He was not alone on a sledge. There was a
line, and he could feel it. It was a line through
hand and eye, block, forge and loom to the
hill. He owned them all: and they owned
him.

"Good-lad-Dick," said Stewart Allman
after the second run, but he didn't offer to
pull the sledge, and the others had lost
interest. William shouted whenever he was
ready to go from the top, and the way was
left clear; but that was all.

The Dorniers came in from the east and
the Heinkels flew overhead. The searchlights swivelled around the sky, but never

saw anything, and the guns began to fire. William watched from the top of the field.

A battery of guns opened up, the flash and then the noise. Everybody stopped sledging when the shrapnel began to fall. It was easier to find on Lizzie Leah's than it was in the village. The fragments zipped and fizzed into the snow. William collected until his pockets were full. He needn't have swapped his incendiary. He had more shrapnel than he could keep.

The others soon began sledging again.

They were having pack races to the gate. If everybody arrived at the same time it was a calamity. If someone got there first but lost control, he had to escape from his own crash before he was hit by the rest.

William pushed off from the top when he heard Stewart Allman shout, "On your marks!" At "Get set!" he was lying back. By "Go!" he was coming down at thirty miles an hour, the spray from his heels hitting his face like freezing sand. He curved round the pack on a new course, and cut in to beat them to the hump. The moment in the air was worth any climb.

He found he could leave at "Get set!" and still have the freedom of the gate. To wait until "Go!" was dangerous.

William was holding on his heels for the next run when he saw how like bombers the pack were in their tight group. He started off. They had opened formation by the time he reached them.

He came in on the bombers from above and out of the sun. Two crossed his sights and he gave them a burst. They went down together. Another tried to dodge him, and crashed. He raced through the pack and settled on the leader's tail. The leader climbed hard at the hump, but William caught his fusilage with a runner and the leader spun out of control and hit the tree.

William landed. The leader was struggling in a thorn hedge. "You're flaming crackers, you are!" said Stewart Allman.

"Look what you've done!"

The field really was littered. The sledge had sent the pack careering all ends up.

"I didn't mean to," said William. "I was a Spitfire."

"He was only being a Spitfire!" Stewart Allman shouted. He limped over to the dump and dropped his broken sledge. "And I've got a sprained Heinkel."

"I didn't mean it," said William.

"Come on, you daft oddment," said Stewart Allman. "We were packing in now, anyroad. That shrapnel's brogged the snow. It's busting the sledges."

"Mine's all right," said William.

"Well, ours aren't," said Stewart Allman. "But play again tomorrow, when it's snowed."

"Play again," said William. "I told you that black cloud was snow."

"It wasn't," said Stewart Allman.

"It was!"

"It wasn't."

"It snowed a blizzard!" said William.

"Yes, but that wasn't the cloud."

"Where did the blizzard come from, then?"

"Out of the sky," said Stewart Allman. "The white bits."

"But the cloud went at the same time as the blizzard," said William.

"That's why," said Stewart Allman. "There was a wind in the cloud, and it blew the snow away. Now there's a proper snow cloud for you."

He pointed to the north. The moon shone on billows, reflecting light. "See, clever-clogs?"

"Play again," said William.

"Play again."

William set off for home. The guns were still firing. Stewart Allman had been right. It was going to snow.

He came to Grandad's house. There was a bicycle propped against the wall. The Air Raid Warden often called for a cup of tea if it wasn't too late in the night.

The sledge runners had taken such a polish that the sledge kept banging William's ankles; so when he stopped he had to swing the rope past him in an arc.

There was more than one bicycle. There were several, against the wall under the thatch. William pulled the sledge up the path and lodged it by the door. He opened the door, went in and closed it, and drew the blackout curtain aside.

The room was empty, but the lamp was lit. There were too many unexpected smells: facepowder, whisky, cigarette smoke. But the room was empty. William listened. He felt and heard the house heavy above him. Nobody was talking, but there was a weight in the room overhead.

Lamplight and shadow were on the bent stairs. William climbed up until he could see.

The bedroom was thatched rafters down to the floor, and it was full of people, still wearing their coats, and standing, pressed by the roof, around Grandad's bed.

William worked between the gathered legs towards the bed.

Voices were whispering, and he was sure he knew the people, but now they were figures darkening him.

He moved a coat hem, and looked straight into Grandad's eyes. The blue eyes and the sharp nose. There was such a clearness in the eyes that William felt that they were speaking to him. Of all the people crowded there, Grandad looked only at William. He must be speaking to him.

"Grandad."

The eyes answered with their fierce blue.

"Grandad, I've been up Lizzie Leah's, and it's a belter. The irons have got a right polish on them now." Someone turned against William as he was kneeling. Grandad sighed, or spoke. "What, Grandad?"

The fierce, kind eyes were still urgent, but that small movement had taken William out of their sight. They were looking at what was before them, at nothing more.

William pushed away from the bed. The coats fell like a curtain. He went backwards to the stairs, and down.

It was a big room. He had never known it empty. William stood in the room and listened to the weight in the house up-ended. All in the bedroom, no one below. The table cleared, but with sawdust in the cracks.

William stood at the chimney. He saw the corner cupboard, the chair.

He spilled the shrapnel across the floor, and when he was rid of it and had only the key in the pocket, the pipe in the tin, he reached into the darkness, and closed his hands.

"Tom Fobble's Day!"

William held the two gleaming horse-shoes.

"No back bargains!"

He ran from the house. The horseshoes

pulled his jacket out of shape, but their weight was light as he ran with his sledge to the top of Lizzie Leah's.

The line did hold. Through hand and eye, block, forge and loom to the hill and all that he owned, he sledged sledged sledged for the black and glittering night and the sky flying on fire and the expectation of snow.